Grace woke up when a heavy hand clamped down over her mouth and a thick voice said, "Don't move a muscle."

The man kept his hand over her mouth while another man used duct tape to bind her feet together. Another piece across her mouth, then they flipped her over and taped her hands together behind her back.

Grace didn't struggle. These men were the size of small cars; fighting them wouldn't do a bit of good. Quietly, quietly, they carried her through the house. How could such big men move so silently? Why didn't someone else in the house wake up and start screaming? Or call the police?

Outside, the wind had picked up and the hem of Grace's baby-doll nightgown fluttered briskly as they crossed the street. The man holding her dumped her unceremoniously into the backseat of the car, and both men got into the front seat. Lightning flashed and in the glare, Grace saw that one of the men was looking at her. She tried to imprint his face on her memory from just that split-second view.

Then suddenly she wanted to scream. The men hadn't blindfolded her, which meant that they were sure she wasn't going to live long enough to ever pick them out of a line-up.

Look for these titles in the **Ocean City** series:

Ocean City
Love Shack
Fireworks
Boardwalk
Ocean City Reunion
Heat Wave
Bonfire
Swept Away
Shipwrecked
Beach Party
Ocean City Forever

And don't miss

**BOYFRIENDS
GIRLFRIENDS**

Katherine Applegate's romantic new series!

#1 Zoey Fools Around
#2 Jake Finds Out
#3 Nina Won't Tell
#4 Ben's In Love
#5 Claire Gets Caught
#6 What Zoey Saw
#7 Lucas Gets Hurt
#8 Aisha Goes Wild

FOREVER

Katherine Applegate

HarperPaperbacks
A Division of HarperCollins*Publishers*

This is a work of fiction. The characters, incidents, and dialogues are products of the author's imagination and are not to be construed as real. Any resemblance to actual events or persons, living or dead, is entirely coincidental.

HarperPaperbacks *A Division of* HarperCollins*Publishers*
10 East 53rd Street, New York, N.Y. 10022

Copyright © 1995 by Daniel Weiss Associates, Inc., and Katherine Applegate
Cover art copyright © 1995 Daniel Weiss Associates, Inc.

All rights reserved. No part of this book may be used or reproduced in any manner whatsoever without written permission of the publisher, except in the case of brief quotations embodied in critical articles and reviews. For information address Daniel Weiss Associates, Inc., 33 West 17th Street, New York, New York 10011.

First printing: July 1995

Printed in the United States of America

HarperPaperbacks and colophon are trademarks of HarperCollins*Publishers*

❖ 10 9 8 7 6 5 4 3 2 1

A special thanks to Katherine Heiny for her help in preparing this manuscript.

OCEAN CITY
FOREVER

ONE

Connor Riordan sprinted along the street toward his apartment, his heart pounding like a triphammer.

A fire! Allegra had said something incoherent about a fire—an emergency—at the apartment, and he had dropped everything and rushed out of his writers' group in the middle of saying something profound. Well, it might have been profound if he'd been able to finish saying it. But when Allegra said *fire*, Connor heard *manuscript*, he heard *charred paper*, he heard *ashes*, as in everything he'd worked for going up in smoke.

Sweat stained the back of Connor's shirt. He reached the house and pounded up the stairs.

Why, *why* hadn't he made of copy of his

manuscript and tucked it somewhere safe, like at Justin's, like in a bank, like in Fort Knox? Was he that cheap? That lazy? For want of a roll of quarters and a Xerox machine, he was racing to save his life—or at least his life's work.

Connor entered his apartment in the manner and velocity of a human cannonball. He nearly knocked Allegra over.

He grabbed her by the shoulders and shook her. "Where is it?" he screamed. "Did you save it? Did you?"

Allegra rolled her eyes. "Unhand me, please. Did I save what?"

"My book!" Connor shouted. "For the love of God, woman, my book! From the fire—" Connor broke off suddenly. He dropped his hands from Allegra's shoulders and looked around. His apartment looked normal. It looked *perfectly* normal. He sniffed the air cautiously. No smoke.

"Where is the fire?" he asked in a calmer, more suspicious tone.

Allegra looked distinctly uncomfortable. "I—"

"You did mean the fire was *here*, right?" Connor said. "You didn't call me out of my writers' group because you, oh, saw a fire on the news, or heard about a fire on the radio?

Or do you have something else in mind? Are you and I going to go bucket-to-bucket with the Ocean City Volunteer Firemen?"

Allegra lifted her chin. "As a matter of fact, I did have something else in mind, Connor." She smiled. Part of Connor's overheated brain noticed that Allegra was wearing a very short white silk robe.

"So," he said uncertainly. "There is no fire? Can we just get that smallest of details straight?"

"Oh, there's a fire," Allegra said softly. "Right here." Then she dropped her shoulder, letting the sleeve of the robe slip off her bare arm, pulling at the belt and letting that drop, then the rest, inch by inch, until the robe lay in a puddle of white silk at her feet.

Oh, please, Allegra thought as the robe rustled to the floor with a slight crushing sound. *Oh, please, let this work. What am I thinking? This will work—this always works*.

Connor was staring at her with his mouth open. Allegra stifled the impulse to shake him. Maybe she'd made a mistake, telling him there was a fire, but how was she to know he'd come tearing across town like Paul Revere spreading the word?

Besides, she'd had to work quickly, because she knew that stupid Chelsea was

3

planning her big reunion and lovefest for tonight. Well, at least she, Allegra, appeared to be in time. Now if she could just get Connor *moving*, things would take their natural course. And if all went according to her plan, she wouldn't have to move out of the apartment—Connor would be asking her to stay.

"Connor," she said softly, gently. She stepped closer to him and wrapped her arms around his neck. If only he didn't look so half-witted and scared to death. *Close your mouth or the gnats will fly in*, she thought sourly. Aloud, she said, "I've wanted this ever since I first laid eyes on you."

And she pressed her richly tanned, perfumed body against him.

Chelsea's heart was as light as a bubble as she skipped toward the apartment. She carried a bag of groceries balanced on one hip and gripped a bottle of sparkling grape drink, but she barely noticed her burdens.

Connor didn't sleep with Jannah! she thought over and over. *And when I tell him that I didn't go to bed with Antonio—why, we'll have no more problems! For the first time in our married life, we'll have no problems!*

Chelsea opened the door of the apartment building and looked at the stairs. Normally

4

she hated these stairs. She hated coming home from work tired and having to plod her slow way up them. But tonight she only laughed.

She hefted the bag of groceries higher on her hip and grasped the bottle more firmly. She drew a deep breath and then took the stairs as fast as she could, two at a time.

The light from the television screen filled Wilton's condo like a thin blue cloud. The sound was off. On the couch, Grace tightened her arms around Wilton's neck and squeezed him for a second.

Wilton stopped kissing her and smiled. She smiled back at him. "Are you okay?" she whispered. "Happy?"

Wilton sat up straighter. "Happy?" he said. "*Happy*? This is only the single greatest day of my life."

"Better than when you won the spelling bee in the third grade?" Grace asked.

"Oh, yeah, lots better. . . . Hey, how'd you know about that?"

"Lucky guess," Grace said, laughing. She ran a hand through her hair.

Wilton kissed her quickly. "In high school I was on this quiz show called *High-Q*, and my team made it through the semifinals and the—Stop laughing, Grace."

"Sorry."

"Yeah, well, I led my team to victory after rousing victory, all the way to the state finals, and we won that too because I answered the final question! *I answered the final question!*" His face was shining with remembered glory.

Grace tried so hard not to laugh that her stomach muscles ached. "What was the question?" she asked.

Wilton shook himself out of his reverie. "Well, my point was that even that moment— the moment when I correctly answered the final question—was not as great as *this* moment." He leaned over to kiss her, but her laughter was unstoppable now.

"Wilton, what was the question?"

"Hey, I'm trying to be romantic here and tell you that you mean more to me than even my stirring triumph over—"

"*What was the question!*"

"Oh, all right," Wilton sighed. "The question was: Name the chemical components of ethylene glycol."

"And you knew that? What were you, a chemistry whiz?"

"No, my brother was, though. He had a miniature laboratory set up in our basement and he used to concoct all sorts of strange substances. Of course, I was his lab assistant, so that question on *High-Q* was a piece of cake for me."

"I didn't know you had a brother—"

"Listen, I'm thirsty," Wilton said, standing up. "Can I get you something? A soda?"

"Ummm, sure." Grace stretched. "Hey, where's the bathroom?"

Wilton pointed. "Just down there on your left." He went into the kitchen.

Grace brushed her hair and reapplied lipstick in the bathroom, the bright lights hurting her eyes after the dim, soft atmosphere of the living room. As she walked back down the hall, she paused at the door of Wilton's bedroom.

Grace smiled as she noticed that all four walls were lined with books. She entered hesitantly. There was a neatly made single bed in the middle of the room and a small desk covered with notebooks, also in the middle of the room. Grace smiled. Wilton obviously hadn't wanted to give up any wall space that might be used for bookshelves.

She ran her fingers lightly along the spines of the books, wondering absently if Wilton had a trophy from *High-Q* and, if so, where it was displayed. She paused.

One of the books, *Naked Lunch*, by William Burroughs, was sticking out slightly. Automatically, she tried to push it back into

7

alignment with the others. It moved partway in and then stopped gently, as though lodged against something soft. A paperback must have fallen back there. Grace removed *Naked Lunch* and reached behind it.

"What are you *doing*?" Wilton shrieked from the doorway.

Grace jumped, and hastily replaced the book. "Just admiring your library," she said.

Beads of sweat stood out on Wilton's forehead. He was carrying two glasses of ginger ale, and the ice in the glasses tinkled as his hands shook.

"Hey, Wilton, I'm sorry," Grace said, stepping toward him. "I wasn't snooping, honest. I was just looking at the books."

"It's okay," Wilton said unsteadily. He set the glasses down on his desk.

Grace thought of the notebooks on the desk and wondered if Wilton was keeping a journal or making notes for a novel. That would certainly explain why he was being such a nervous Nellie.

She put her arms around him. "Hey, it really is okay," she said.

Wilton kissed the top of her head. "Sorry I freaked out."

"Don't be silly. I shouldn't have come in here, but I was curious."

"Curious?" Wilton ran his hands down her back.

"Well, yeah, I want to know all about you. All your deep dark secrets."

"I don't have any secrets," Wilton said firmly.

"Oh, everyone has secrets." Grace stood on tiptoe and kissed his chin.

"Not me," Wilton said, and kissed her again before she could say anything else.

Kate and Justin sat on the beach behind Grace's house.

"Who would've ever thought I'd want to sit on the beach and look at the ocean again?" Kate said. "When we were stranded on the island, all I could think about were hot showers and soft beds and tall frosty glasses of iced tea."

Justin put his arm around her shoulders. "The lap of luxury," he said. "Well, maybe the lap of technology."

"Definitely," Kate nodded. "I never want to be without a radio or a telephone or a walkie-talkie again."

"Well, we're safe now," Justin said.

"Mmm." She rested her head on his shoulder. "Hey, did I tell you that Chelsea and Connor are getting back together?"

"Hey, that's great. I'm all in favor of true

love," Justin said. He kissed the tip of Kate's nose and then, very gently, her lips. "Wait a minute, though," he said suddenly, sitting up. "If Chelsea moves back into the apartment, where will Allegra go?"

"Who cares?" Kate said, exasperated.

"Well, I care because she might try to weasel her way back into our lives," Justin said. "She might try to destroy our house or something, like she destroyed the *Kate*."

"I see what you mean," Kate said. "We are the only people she knows in Ocean City, lucky us."

"Boy, when I think of the stunts she pulled on the island . . ."

"Tell me about it," Kate said bitterly.

"She's so—so—"

"Evil? Manipulative? Sharklike?" Kate laughed shortly. "I think they all apply."

"Yeah, they all pretty much do," Justin said. "But the word I was thinking of is calculating. She never gets tired of lying, or of thinking up new lies and schemes. She'll never just break down and tell the truth. And she'll never—" He paused.

"Never what?"

"She'll never be trustworthy."

Kate rolled her eyes. "Have you just figured that out? Well, thanks for the late-breaking news flash, but I could have told you that long ago."

Justin shrugged. "Trustworthy isn't what I mean, exactly. It's just that sometimes I think Allegra would rather get what she wants by conning, even if the honest way were easier."

They were both silent for a moment, and then Justin said, "I've been kind of worried about Allegra wreaking havoc over at Connor's ever since I took her over there."

"Yes, I worried about that, too," Kate said. "But really, what's she going to do?"

Connor was so tall that even standing on tiptoe, Allegra could only kiss his collarbone. She tried to do that as seductively as possible, but Connor only cleared his throat loudly.

"Listen," he said. "I never thought I'd say this to a beautiful naked girl in my own kitchen, but—Would you mind getting dressed and going home?"

Allegra frowned. "This *is* my home," she said as she picked up her silky robe and slipped it on, cinching the belt around her thin waist.

"Oh, yeah. Well, okay, would you mind getting dressed and going to somebody else's home?"

"Connor—"

"I'm serious," Connor said. "Look, I'm flattered as can be—"

"So then what's the problem?"

Connor began ticking them off on his fingers. "I'm married, I love my wife, I don't love you, in fact I don't know you—"

"But I could make you love me!" Allegra said. "I know I could!"

"You aren't listening to me." Connor stopped. Tears were filling Allegra's green eyes. "Oh, for God's sake."

She sniffled and buried her face against his narrow chest.

"This is not going to work," Connor announced. "This is most definitely not going to work."

"Oh, how can you be so mean!" Allegra cried into his shirt.

"Because I—"

Crash!

There was a sudden thundering sound, and Connor and Allegra jumped apart.

Chelsea stood in the doorway, a green glass bottle in splinters at her feet.

"Chelsea," Connor began, but Allegra interrupted him.

"Chelsea, oh my God, I never wanted you to find out this way."

"Find out what?" Chelsea and Connor said together.

Allegra looked a little disconcerted. "About us," she said, gesturing at Connor.

"There is no us," Connor said. "I don't know why you keep talking as if there is." He turned to Chelsea. "What are you doing here?"

Chelsea looked at Connor, then Allegra, then back at Connor. "I had to talk to you," she said softly.

"With a bag of groceries?" Connor said. He nudged a piece of broken glass with his foot. "And a bottle of—"

"Sparkling grape drink." Chelsea pushed a stray lock of hair out of her face. "I thought we could—" She broke off suddenly and turned to Allegra. "Look, do you think you could possibly *go* somewhere? I'd like to talk to Connor."

"Are you insane?" Allegra asked mildly, leaning against the kitchen counter. "You walk in and find your husband in the arms of another woman and you don't ask any questions? I think it should be obvious what's going on, even to you."

"Even to me?"

"Well, the wife is always the last to know."

"I see," Chelsea said evenly. "Well, I must admit that I was somewhat startled to find you wearing that skimpy robe, but then

13

again, I don't know you, Allegra. Maybe that's how you do housework or something."

"Housework—"

"And I don't think you were exactly in Connor's arms, were you? Besides, *he* has all his clothes on. Not to mention that about five minutes ago I saw him make a mad dash out of the building where his writers' group meets. So how *did* you lure him away from his meeting, Allegra?"

"She said there was a fire," Connor piped up.

"Well, there you are," Chelsea said easily. "Now, if you don't mind, Connor and I really do need to talk. Why don't you go . . . do whatever it is you do."

"But where am I supposed to—"

"To stay? Gosh, I don't know," Chelsea said. "Certainly not here, though. Unless you have any objections, Connor, I think I'll be staying here tonight."

Connor looked into Chelsea's eyes. "No objections," he said softly.

Chelsea smiled. "Good," she said, pushing him gently into the kitchen. Over her shoulder, she said, "Oh, Allegra, be sure to pack up your—clothes, for lack of a better word."

Allegra opened her mouth and then closed it with a snap. She snatched up her

14

duffel bag, then spun on her heel and marched into the bathroom.

"Shouldn't we watch her to make sure she doesn't pack the family silver?" Connor said.

"We don't have any silver," Chelsea laughed.

"True . . ." Connor put his arms around her. "Hey, you surprised me in there."

"I surprised myself," Chelsea said. "But Connor, there have been so many misunderstandings between us already. Don't you think it's about time we started trusting each other and just concentrated on being happy?"

"But Antonio—Jannah—I thought—"

"I only let you think that about me and Antonio because I thought you and Jannah—"

"Oh, God, we never did anything!"

"I know that. But I *did* kiss Antonio, Connor," Chelsea said seriously.

"And that's it?"

"That's it."

"Well, I told you I could live with a kiss, Chels. I'm not thrilled about it, but it doesn't mean we have to get divorced, for God's sake. Besides, you told me about it and that means a lot to me."

"Oh, Connor," Chelsea said, slipping her arms around his neck. "I feel so happy. I feel like I could cure cancer or fly to the moon or run the Boston Marathon."

Connor winced. "I feel like I already ran the Boston Marathon. I don't think I've ever run so fast."

"Well, I've certainly never seen you run that fast. It looked like your head was going to snap off."

Connor pretended to scowl. "What does that mean, young lady?" He backed her against the counter.

Chelsea giggled. "I don't know. It's just that you were tearing along and your body was moving faster than your neck, I guess, because your head was sort of *hanging*—Connor, hey, take your hands off me, we have to clean up the mess in there."

"Later," Connor said, kissing her temple.

"I mean it, it's going to look like somebody was *killed* unless we try to scrub the floor now."

"Later." Connor unbuttoned the top three buttons on her blouse.

Chelsea laughed. "Did I tell you how much I paid for all this food? Unbelievable."

"Later," Connor said. "Tell me later."

"Connor—" Chelsea began, but Connor kissed her and she forgot all about her groceries and the broken glass and the stain on the floor. And neither of them heard Allegra slam out of the apartment a minute later.

Two

Grace glided up the walk to her house in slow motion. She felt exactly the way she felt after swimming: relaxed to the point of pleasant tiredness, buoyed by the exercise, and slightly disoriented from having existed temporarily in another medium.

Kate was sitting at the kitchen table, angrily stirring a cup of tea. She glanced at Grace and said, "Oh, my God."

Grace ran her fingers over her face and hair vaguely. "What? Do I have something on my face?"

Kate smiled. "Just a stupid, sort of lovesick expression."

"Lovesick?" Grace repeated, horrified.

Kate nodded. "And you were humming."

"I was not."

"Yes, you were. 'Beautiful Dreamer.' I know because I had to play that for my sixth-grade piano recital. So, come on, who's the guy? He must be pretty wonderful."

Grace thought privately that if Wilton heard a girl as beautiful and smart as Kate assume that he was "pretty wonderful," he would be even happier than when he soared to victory on *High-Q*, or whatever the show was.

"Well, *I* think he's wonder—pretty nice," she said cautiously. She sat down across the table from Kate.

"Marta told me that you and Carr were having a big thing," Kate said, "but since he hightailed it back to Kansas to be with his girlfriend, it can't be him."

Grace sighed. "No, Carr and I had a small thing, a nonexistent thing. We tried to get something going, but he was just too connected to Jody. So connected that he couldn't even make it through the summer without her." Grace paused, then said, "This is someone else, Kate. . . . His name is Wilton."

"Try to sound a little more excited."

Grace glanced up from the tabletop and caught Kate's eye. "I am excited, Kate. That's the whole thing. I do think Wilton's wonderful, but—"

"But what?"

"But—you and Justin and everyone might not think so."

Kate laughed, startling Grace. "Oh, please," she said.

"What?"

"As if we don't think enough of you to like whoever it is that you like! Give me a break."

Grace watched Kate with amazement. Is this the girl with whom she used to have trouble exchanging two civil words in a row?

She smiled back at Kate. "Hey, what are you doing up, anyway? You look like you should be pacing back and forth with a rolling pin."

Kate frowned into her teacup. "Chelsea called a little while ago and told me that Allegra was up to her old tricks, and that she and Connor have thrown her out of the apartment."

"What old tricks?"

"Well, I didn't really find out, because all Chelsea said was something about Allegra doing her best to drive a wedge between Chelsea and Connor, and then Connor picked up the extension and said 'Chels, come into the bedroom, I want to show you something,' in this really corny voice, and then he growled and they both started laughing like mad and hung up. So at any rate, I figure Allegra will show here any time now."

19

"Did you say Connor *growled*?" Grace said.

"Yeah, you should have heard it. He sounded like a werewolf."

There was a soft knocking at the kitchen door.

Kate and Grace looked at each other. "Right on cue," Kate said, and Grace called, "Come in."

Allegra stepped tentatively into the kitchen. "Oh, thank God you're up," she whispered. "I saw the light was on."

"We've been expecting you," Kate said.

Allegra looked wary. "You have? Why?"

"Chelsea called."

A momentary expression flickered across Allegra's face, but Grace saw it: disappointment. Allegra recovered herself swiftly though, and now her only expression was one of sincerity. "Kate, you have to believe me," she said earnestly. "Chelsea misunderstood—"

"Oh, I have to believe you, do I?" Kate said, leaning back in her chair. "I *have* to believe you over my best friend who I've known and trusted for years? But then, you certainly did prove yourself trustworthy on the island, didn't you?"

"Kate, honest—" Allegra began.

"What did you try, anyway? Did you leave

your underpants in Connor's bed? Put lipstick on his shirt collar?"

"I never—"

Kate picked up a pen that someone had left lying on the table and scribbled something on a paper napkin. She handed the napkin to Grace.

"I just seem to do everything wrong," Allegra was saying, her lovely green eyes starting to shimmer with unshed tears. "I try, but nothing . . ." She paused and sniffled. "What does that say?" she asked Grace.

Grace cleared her throat. "It says, 'Here come the waterworks.'"

Allegra blinked and the tears were gone. It happened so swiftly and completely that Grace was fascinated. She wanted to ask Allegra to do it again.

"Look," Allegra said. "I know what you think of me, but I have nowhere else to go. What are you going to do, turn me out in the middle of the night?"

"Why not?" Kate asked. She was still sitting back in her chair, looking relaxed, but her blue eyes were cold. "Why should we take you in, Allegra? You repaid our original charity by wrecking the *Kate*. You're going to say we should give you a second chance, but we already have. We've given you chance after chance, and it never leads to anything but more of your 'misunderstandings.' " She stood up. "I have to go to bed now, so if you don't mind . . ." She gestured toward the door.

Allegra bit her lip. She appeared undecided, but then she sighed. "Okay, okay," she said. She walked slowly out the door and down the steps to the beach.

Grace got up to shut the door behind her.

Kate began turning out the lights. "That girl . . ." She shook her head. "What a piece of work."

"Mmm," Grace said vaguely. She was watching Allegra through the window. Allegra was walking slowly and idly toward the boardwalk. Suddenly she glanced behind her and, seeing Grace, squared her shoulders and began walking more steadily, pretending she had someplace to go.

Allegra walked down the beach in the moonlight, trying to decide what she felt the worst about. There were so many things! Allegra had the horrible feeling that for the rest of her life, she would wake up every morning and have one second of happiness before she thought *Oh, no, what am I supposed to be worrying about?*

Right now, of course, she didn't even

know *where* she'd wake up tomorrow, so maybe she should worry about that. She supposed she could sleep under the boardwalk. But this wasn't the Bahamas, and she was starting to feel chilled. And what if she was attacked or killed by a wino or something while trying to sleep on the beach?

Oh, why had she ever pulled that stupid stunt with Connor? She'd known that she was staying at his apartment on a strictly probational basis, just as she knew she wasn't welcome at the big house, either. But—but, well, she'd had to do *something*, right? And it wasn't like she'd felt *terrific* about trying to destroy Connor's marriage to what's-her-name, Kate's friend. At least that girl had seemed about a zillion times mellower and less judgmental than Kate.

Allegra shuddered as the evening's events raced through her mind. Kate had been so—so happy, so satisfied. And that other woman, the gorgeous dark-eyed one, had looked like she had wanted to disappear. Why, Allegra had almost been *ashamed*.

Now, if I just had some money, I could shake the dust of this town from my shoes forever, Allegra thought bitterly. *But I don't have any money because someone—guess who?— skedaddled with my cocaine.*

Sand had worked its way into Allegra's sandals, and she sat down to shake it out. She was so tired.

So who did have the drugs, the beloved drugs that she'd risked life and limb for to smuggle them past the Coast Guard? *Yeah, thanks a lot, whoever you are*, she thought. She tried to think. Well, she knew who it *wasn't*: Kate, Justin, Connor, any of that gang. They were all too uptight—they would've called the police in five seconds. Someone had left her that note: *Don't be afraid, we'll work it out.* She knew it wasn't Chernak, because Chernak's note would have read, *You better be afraid, because I'm going to get you when you least expect it*—or something like that.

Allegra shivered a little just imagining it. Chernak *would* get her if she ever gave him half a chance. She hadn't the tiniest doubt about it. So where was he, anyway? Had he paid someone to steal the coke and leave a note, lulling her into a false sense of security? Well, that didn't make much sense, and besides—

A hand fell on Allegra's shoulder, and she shrieked, leaping to her feet.

"Hey, take it easy," said a voice. "I didn't mean to scare you."

Allegra turned and saw the girl from the beach house, the pretty one with big dark eyes, what was her name—Greta? No . . . Grace. She was standing there, holding out a sweatshirt.

"I brought this for you," she said simply. "It's getting cold."

Allegra looked at her suspiciously, but the brown eyes were unreadable. "Thanks," she said at last, taking the sweatshirt and slipping it over her head.

"You're welcome," Grace said. "I brought this for you, too." She pressed a roll of bills into Allegra's hand. "There's a motel up by the bus station—you know where that is? It's called the Seaside. I think they rent rooms by the week. It's kind of a dump, but I don't think you'll be murdered in your bed or anything."

She turned and began walking back toward the house.

Allegra stared at the money in her hand for a minute. "Hey, wait!" she called. "Hey! Grace!"

Grace turned around and looked at her. "Yes?" she asked. The wind blew a strand of dark hair across her face, and she reached up and tucked it behind her ear.

Allegra took a few steps closer to her.

"Thank you so much," she said. "I'll pay you back every cent, I swear."

Grace shrugged. "If you like," she said. "Good night." She started walking again.

"*Wait!*" Allegra cried.

Grace turned again. She raised her eyebrows.

"At least tell me why you're being so nice," Allegra said. "I mean, especially after Kate was so mean to me. Or—is that it? Do you hate Kate or something?"

"Oh, please," Grace snapped. Her eyebrows drew together. "I happen to like Kate very much, but even if I did hate her, I wouldn't do something just to spite her. Not everything has to be so cause-and-effect—so calculating and sly."

"But then . . ." Allegra faltered.

"Look," Grace said. "I could sense a desperation about you, and I happen to know something about desperation. And then when I was watching you through the window, you—you squared your shoulders in this way that . . . I don't know. I guess maybe it made me think you weren't such a lost cause after all."

Grace looked thoughtful for a moment, then began walking again. Allegra caught her arm.

"But if I'm not a lost cause, why won't you tell me why you're doing this?" she said.

"I *did* tell you," Grace said.

"But—but—" Allegra struggled. "What do you know about desperation?"

Grace sighed. "I'm an alcoholic, Allegra, and that's not so different from being a con, which seems to be what you are." She glanced up at Allegra as if expecting an argument, but Allegra just looked intrigued. "So don't make this into something it's not. I helped you out tonight, but that doesn't mean I like you, or approve of you, or that I'll help you in the future. You may well keep doing the same things over and over. I just don't know."

"But what is it that you hope I'll do?" Allegra said.

Grace smiled sarcastically. "Oh, I always hope everyone will do the right thing in the end. Now, please, let go of my arm."

Allegra let go. She watched Grace walk away, her gait smooth and carefree, her hands clasped behind her back.

"Good-bye!" Allegra called. "Good-bye, Grace!"

But either the wind was too loud or Grace was tired of talking, because she didn't turn around.

• • •

Kate lay with her head on Justin's chest, listening to his heart beat.

"So, you think Allegra's really gone?" he asked.

"Well, she's not here, and she's not at Chelsea and Connor's, that's for sure," Kate said. "Where else does she have to go?"

"I don't know. . . . I guess she could go down to the marina and proposition a sailor or something."

"Mmm . . . let's wish her well, then," Kate said sleepily.

Justin laughed softly. "Just as long as she doesn't come back here." He paused. "Did I just hear Grace come in? Did she go out?"

Kate buried her face in his chest. "No, she was out earlier with some guy. . . ."

"Who?" Justin asked, but Kate didn't answer. Her breathing was deep and regular. "Hey," he said gently. "Am I boring you?"

Kate stirred. "Mmm," she said. "We need our sleep."

"True," Justin said, stroking her hair. "We have to go back to being lifeguards tomorrow." He spoke slowly, thoughtfully. "I'm kind of looking forward to it. I could use some order and routine after everything we've been through."

"Me, too," Kate said, surprising him. "And anyway, what can happen to us here?"

Grace tiptoed into the bathroom, easing the door shut behind her. She washed her face and brushed her teeth slowly, lost in thought about Wilton.

Changing in the darkness of her room, she put on a nightgown and climbed into bed. She lay there, staring dreamily at the ceiling. Grace couldn't put her finger on it, but something was bothering her—something about the way Wilton had acted earlier.

She rolled onto her side. He'd been so defensive when he'd found her in his room. Well, maybe he's just a hard person to get close to, she thought, although that doesn't really fit with the Wilton she knew. And he certainly wasn't possessive of his books—just the opposite, in fact. So why had he been so bothered by her perusing his bookshelves? Then the rest of the night he'd seemed so distracted and distant, Grace almost got the feeling that he wanted her to leave.

Grace sighed and rearranged her pillows. What was she expecting—a proposal? Hadn't he told her that tonight was the greatest night of his life? And now she thought he was *distant*.

She finally settled down, hugging one of the pillows. *I am not pretending this is Wilton*, she thought. *I just want to set the record straight*. But she was smiling when she fell asleep.

Connor sat in bed, propped up on pillows. Chelsea sat facing him, holding a plate piled high with scrambled eggs. She took turns feeding him and then herself.

"Wow, these are the best eggs in the world," Connor said with his mouth full.

Chelsea giggled and kissed his nose. "You said the same thing about the macaroni and cheese, and about the chicken noodle soup, and even about that *extremely* questionable steak that I found in the refrigerator."

"Hey, that was a great piece of steak," Connor protested.

"Yes, I'm sure it was perfectly delicious when it made its dinner party debut back in 1972," Chelsea said. "I still can't believe you ate that. There's no telling how old it was."

Connor took the empty plate and set it on the nightstand. He nuzzled Chelsea's neck. "I can't help it. I eat when I'm happy."

"Me, too," Chelsea said. "Of course, I also eat when I'm unhappy. That's why my hips look the way they do."

"I love your hips," Connor said softly. "They're perfect hips, perfect—Hey, where are you going?"

"Connor, let me go, I have to clean up the mess in the kitchen or some sort of toxic *cloud* is going to form in there. Hey! Connor! Oh, let me up!" she shrieked as Connor pulled her back onto the bed.

"Later," he said, grinning.

"That's what you've been saying all night," Chelsea said. Then she screamed as he tickled her.

"Quiet," Connor whispered in her ear. "You'll wake the neighbors."

They never did get around to cleaning the kitchen, or the spilled grape drink, that night. As Chelsea predicted, the ominous-looking crimson stain would mark the spot forever, mystifying all future tenants of that apartment.

Allegra hoped that Grace knew what she was talking about when she said that Allegra wouldn't be murdered in her bed at the Seaside Motel.

She lay still as a stick on the damp, lumpy mattress, straining her ears for sounds, fearing that at any moment she'd hear someone rattling the doorknob. She thought bitterly that all you'd have to do was *look* at the motel room door hard enough and it would fly open, it was so thin and cheaply constructed.

Next door, Allegra's neighbor was playing a guitar and singing country-and-western songs. Nearly all the songs were about men getting out of prison or dogs getting run over or pickup trucks breaking down. And every single song mentioned a cheap motel.

Allegra sighed and relaxed her vigil. How had she ever come to such an end? She wasn't meant to pass the night in cheap motels listening to drunken guitarists.

But perhaps some part of Allegra felt perfectly at home, because she was fast asleep and snoring sweetly in less than five minutes.

Wilton sat at his desk, rubbing the bridge of his nose and writing in his journal. Normally he wrote an exhaustive account of his day: whom he'd seen, what they'd said, whether his parents were suspicious, whether he'd heard from Eric, whether anyone had had a profound thought, whether he, Wilton, had had a profound thought. The average daily entry was three pages long. Wilton tended to analyze and reanalyze everything that happened to him. Sometimes he thought he did about one minute of actual living for every fifteen minutes of thinking about living.

Tonight he stared at the place on the bookshelf where he'd hidden Allegra's cocaine. Then he stared at the blank page in front of him. He'd written a lot about the coke in the journal, using an informal code based on a recipe in *The Joy of Cooking*.

But tonight he didn't feel like writing. Or rather, he *did* feel like writing, but he was too full of emotions to do so.

After a long time he wrote two sentences very rapidly. Then he switched off the light, crawled into bed, and leaped into sleep. The two sentences he'd written were: *Tonight Grace Caywood kissed me. My heart feels like a balloon.*

THREE

Chelsea woke up the next morning, smelled coffee brewing and bacon frying, and thought *Mother's making breakfast for Daddy*. Then she remembered where she was and she smiled deliciously, sliding further under the covers. No, she thought, that's *Connor* making breakfast for *me*.

As if on cue, Connor appeared a moment later with a plate of bacon and eggs, a mug of coffee, and a dandelion in a Dixie cup all balanced precariously on a cookie sheet.

"Good morning, love," he said, setting the cookie sheet on her lap and sitting on the edge of the bed.

"Oh, Connor," Chelsea said. "This is wonderful!"

Connor snorted. "Yeah, except that I had

to use a cookie sheet for a tray and a weed for a flower."

Chelsea nearly upset the tray leaning to kiss him. "Well, I think it's perfect," she said.

Connor smiled. "Good," he said. "And now, my love, I'm off to my study for a few hours."

"Okay," Chelsea said happily.

Connor went into the next room, and a minute later Chelsea heard the hum of his computer. She smiled. How happy, how idiotically happy she felt. Here she was having breakfast in bed while her loving husband worked in the next room. What could be better than that?

Chelsea finished her breakfast and then wandered into the kitchen to refill her coffee cup. The sight terrified her: a stack of food-encrusted plates towered in the sink, every pot and pan they owned cluttered the counter, glasses nearly opaque with greasy fingerprints were scattered everywhere, and the floor was spattered with samples of everything that had been cooked or eaten in the kitchen for the past two weeks. And Chelsea thought she'd been right about a toxic cloud forming—the air seemed to palpitate with various obnoxious smells, most overwhelmingly bacon grease.

Chelsea sighed. She tiptoed across the floor, refilled her cup, and crept back to the bedroom. She would start straightening up in here first and tackle the kitchen when she felt up to it.

She made the bed lazily, carried a few dishes into the kitchen, and began dusting with a feather duster in a slow, aimless way, humming to herself.

She moved a pile of papers off Connor's nightstand and glanced at the top sheet. A sentence caught her eye: *It was difficult to say who was the better-looking, Jason or Kara, for they were both perfect in their own way, although perhaps Kara's unawareness of her beauty made her all the more lovely.*

Chelsea paused, delighted. This was Connor's novel! She'd always thought he kept it under lock and key in his study, but here it was! Kara and Jason—would that be Kate and Justin? She glanced at the page number: thirty-four. Quickly she shuffled through the pages and began reading on the first page. By the third page, she was utterly absorbed, her coffee growing cool and untouched at her elbow.

By the tenth page, she felt like throwing the manuscript across the room. They were all in there, in thinly disguised pseudonyms: Kara (Kate), Jason (Justin), Colin (Connor),

Charisse (Chelsea), Maida (Marta), Carl (Carr), Casey (Grace—Connor had apparently chosen to rhyme, here), Rose (Roan), D.B. (B.D.), and Beau (Bo).

For heaven's sake, he'd used Bo's actual name, just with a different spelling! And he didn't even bother to make up new initials for B.D., he just switched them around! But it got worse. Chelsea's hands trembled as she read:

> Charisse was not yet a woman, perhaps, but an entrancing girl who projected a sweetness and purity that would have discouraged more carnal thoughts, had it not been that she also possessed a nearly perfect behind that, for Colin, utterly obliterated all consideration of her intellectual and moral attributes.

Chelsea thought she would go up in smoke. So "Kara" had an unawareness of her beauty, making her even lovelier, and "Charisse" just had a great butt? *Oh, wonderful*, Chelsea thought. *He doesn't even say I have a nice personality! He doesn't even say I have a nice face!*

"Chelsea?" Connor called.

Chelsea caught her breath. She swept the

papers back together and replaced them on Connor's nightstand.

"Chels?"

"In here," she called.

Connor appeared in the doorway. "Hey, you're still in your nightgown," he said. "What have you been doing?"

"I got caught up in a good book," Chelsea said, but Connor missed her sarcasm.

"Want to go out to lunch?" he said. "I thought we could celebrate."

"Celebrate what?" Chelsea narrowed her eyes.

"Celebrate what? Our marital bliss, of course!" Connor leaned down and kissed her. "Aren't you happy, doll?"

Chelsea looked into Connor's bright blue eyes and wavered. Maybe she'd misjudged him. After all, the book *was* supposed to be a work of fiction, not an autobiography.

"Yes, I'm happy," she said softly.

"Good." Connor touched the tip of her nose. "Now get dressed, kitten, and we'll go."

He wandered into the kitchen, and Chelsea heard him say, "Yikes!" The mess is even getting to him, she thought.

She drifted over to the closet and pulled a sundress off a hanger. She stood there for a moment, lost in thought. She remembered

Connor last night. *I think your hips are perfect, Chelsea, perfect . . .*

"Chels? You ready?" Connor called.

"In a minute," she answered. Under her breath, she said, "I just have to find something form-fitting enough to make up for my lack of intellectual attributes."

Allegra sat on the beach, her face angry and sullen. *First I had to sleep in that fleabag motel*, she thought bitterly, *and then I spent the morning listening to children scream their heads off.*

That miserable job at the day-care center! Every single kid had a cold and wanted Allegra to blow his or her nose. They wanted Allegra to take them to bathroom. They wanted her to read to them. They wanted to pick imaginary cooties out of her hair. They wanted—Allegra shuddered. She'd worked half the day and then slipped out the back on her lunch break.

She would just have to make the money that Grace had given her last until she could sell the cocaine. She simply couldn't take another minute at the day-care center. But meanwhile she had barely enough money to live on. She couldn't even splurge to buy a soda.

Down the beach she could see Justin's stand, circled by a crowd of girls. Kate's stand was flanked by a similar number of bare-chested men playing volleyball and walking on their hands and doing any stupid antic they could think of to make Kate smile her gentle, beautiful smile.

Huh! Allegra thought. *I'm twice as pretty as she is. In fact, I'm prettier than any of the girls thronging around Justin.*

It was true. Allegra was probably the most beautiful girl on the beach that day. But she was in such a bad mood that her marvelous green eyes only sparked venom, and her lovely full mouth was set in such stubborn lines that none of the guys on the beach felt like approaching her.

Well, that was just as well. She had things to think about. That note, for instance. *Don't be afraid, we'll work it out.* Well, okay. Allegra was certainly ready to work it out. Whatever the mystery thief wanted, fine. She would give anything in order to get out of the Seaside Motel and into the Ocean City Grande or something more suitable. But why had the person left a note? Why did he or she want to work things out *at all*? Why not just take the coke and hightail it? Why not—

"Pardon me," said a voice.

Allegra glanced up. A tall, skinny guy with glasses was standing there, peering down at her with a puppyish expression.

"Scram," Allegra said. She looked back out at the ocean.

"Pardon me," the skinny guy said again.

Allegra looked at him with irritation. "What is it?" she snapped. "Do I look like an information booth?"

"No, I—"

"Then beat it."

"I wanted to talk to you."

"I'm getting married September fifteenth," Allegra said automatically. "Sorry."

And I would never go out with such a sorry-looking specimen as you anyway, she added silently.

"Listen—" he said again.

"No, you listen, guy," Allegra said. "I'm not interested, get it? I'm not buying what you're selling, is that understood?"

"Perfectly." The guy pushed his glasses up his nose. Then he said deliberately, "Don't be afraid. We'll work it out."

Allegra snatched her sunglasses off. "*What*?" she whispered hoarsely. "What did you just say?"

"You heard me."

She leaned back on her blanket and looked

41

the skinny guy up and down. "Well, well, well," she said. "I've been wondering when I'd hear from you."

"Here I am."

"Yes, so I see," Allegra said. "Well, don't expect me to fall all over you in gratitude."

"Oh, I don't expect that," the guy said easily.

"Well, since your note said we could work it out, you obviously expect something," Allegra sighed. "Let me guess. You stole my coke, but you don't have a source, so if I set you up with a buyer, you're willing to cut me in for a fraction of my own money, right?"

"Actually, no."

Allegra raised her eyebrows. "Please don't keep me in suspense."

"Chernak sent me."

Allegra felt a finger of fear slide down her back, but she kept her face blank. Surely nothing was going to happen to her here in broad daylight.

"I'm sure I don't know who you're talking about," she said icily.

"Yes, you do," the guy said. "I know all about you, Allegra. My name is Wilton, by the way."

"Charmed," she said, but he didn't blink.

"Look, I really do want to work something out," Wilton said. "I'm in a jam—Chernak's blackmailing me."

"With what?" Allegra looked at Wilton with new respect. What had he done? Killed someone? Slept with someone's wife?

"My brother Eric is, um, he's in prison, and Chernak says that he can arrange for Eric to have an 'accident' in the prison laundry if I don't do what he says."

"He *can* arrange that, I'm certain," Allegra says. "Don't underestimate him."

"I don't."

"What's your brother in prison for? Murder?"

"Certainly not." Wilton looked offended. "Check forgery. Strictly white-collar crime."

"Goody for him. Your mother must be very proud," Allegra said. "Will you get to the point?"

"Jeez, you're not a very nice person," Wilton said mildly. "Okay. The point is that I don't want to be the one to give the coke to Chernak, because I don't want the miserable extortionist to make a dime off me. Also, Chernak mentioned that he had . . . rather unpleasant plans in store for you. I thought if we worked together, we could destroy the drugs and think up a plausible story to tell him."

Allegra stared. She could not believe her luck.

"Plausible story?" she repeated.

43

"Yeah, like, give him a teeny little bit of cocaine and tell him that's all you could get past the Coast Guard or something."

"I—" Allegra broke off as a two little kids approached. "What?" she said to them.

The bigger little kid pointed at the smaller one. "My brother scraped his elbow." The brother dutifully displayed his scraped elbow. "And we need you to spray some of that stuff on it."

"Oh, for heaven's sake," Allegra said. "Go bother someone else."

"Timmy said he knew you," the kid said. "He said you work at the day-care center."

Allegra sighed. "Well, his elbow doesn't look that bad to me," she said. "Go for a swim in the ocean. Saltwater is the best disinfectant there is. Now, I'm having a very important conversation, so run along."

The kid put his hands on his hips. "Listen," he said, "our mom's a lawyer, and if we tell her you refused to spray Solarcaine on Timmy's arm, she'll have you fired from the day-care center."

Too late, Allegra thought.

The kid was still talking. "And our dad's—"

"Oh, all *right*, I get your point," Allegra snapped. She stood up. Wilton was looking at her like she was some sort of monster. Great.

44

She grabbed each kid by the hand and began dragging them toward the first-aid hut. Over her shoulder, she said, "Wilton, will you wait right here?"

"No, I have to get back to work," Wilton said. "But I'll be in touch."

"Promise?" Allegra said. She had already formed a plan, and it made her so happy that she flashed Wilton a smile and laughed, and the laugh made her green eyes sparkle. She looked so beautiful that Timmy and his brother both fell in love with her.

Kate looked up and gave her first genuine-and-not-just-polite smile of the day. "Chelsea!" she said. "How'd it go last night?"

Chelsea beamed. "Oh, it was wonderful! I—"

Kate held up her hands. "Spare me the gruesome details, please. Hearing Connor growl on the telephone was quite enough for me."

Chelsea laughed, then bit her lip. She seemed on the verge of saying something, but Kate knew better than to push her. Chelsea would say whatever was on her mind when she was ready.

"What brings you down here?" Kate asked.

Chelsea held up a white paper bag.

"Connor and I had barbecued ribs for lunch and I brought you some, in case you were hungry."

"Oh, thank you," Kate said, genuinely pleased. How nice of Chelsea to think of her on the day after she put her marriage back together. Kate called for a replacement, and she and Chelsea stretched out on the sand.

"Mmm, fantastic," Kate said, eating a rib and smearing barbecue sauce on her chin. "So, everything's okay between you and Connor? Really?"

Chelsea nodded. "I even took a couple days off from work to spend time with him." She hesitated. "I—found something this morning . . . but it's probably nothing. Hey, what about you and Justin? You're getting along okay?"

Kate wondered what Chelsea had found. Evidence that Connor was seeing Jannah? Or Allegra? But Chelsea would be more upset. "Oh, better than getting along," she said lightly. "We're in heaven now that we don't have Chernak or Allegra to deal with. Now we can just be . . . ." She hesitated.

"Now you can just be in love," Chelsea finished for her.

"Well, yes," Kate said. Her eyes traveled down the beach to Justin's stand.

Chelsea saw her look. "Is it hard to be in

love with someone who attracts so many girls?" she asked.

Kate shook her head. "I used to think so," she said slowly. "I used to be jealous all the time, but now . . . Justin and I have been through so much. I can't imagine either one of us with someone else."

"So get married," Chelsea said airily, and then stopped when she caught sight of Kate's face. "You've been thinking about it, haven't you?"

Kate looked away, then nodded. "Sometimes," she said. She licked the last of the barbecue sauce from her fingers.

Chelsea grinned. "So do it," she said. She crumpled up the paper bag. "You think there's going to be a perfect time, when you're ready and everything's all set, but it's never like that. . . . So just do it."

Kate laughed. "Listen to you, the wise old voice of reason."

"That's me," Chelsea said. She looked back down at Justin's beach stand. "Look at all those girls," she said. "Maybe it's just as well I married someone who looks like an overgrown leprechaun."

"Hey, Connor," Justin said. "What are you doing?"

Connor tossed him a paper bag. Justin caught it. It felt like it contained the carcass of a small animal. He looked inside cautiously: barbecued ribs.

"Oh, wow," Justin said. "Thanks, man."

"You're welcome," Connor said. He climbed partway up the stand and sat at Justin's feet. "Chelsea took some to Kate, so I thought I'd bring some to you."

"I'm glad you did," Justin said. "Want one?"

"Well, okay, sure," said Connor, who'd just finished lunch. He took a rib and began gnawing on it.

"Listen," Justin said. "Kate told me that Allegra tried to pull something. . . . I'm really sorry about sticking you with her."

"Oh, yeah! Don't do me any more favors," Connor said, but he didn't seem angry.

"Did she make a pass at you?"

"That's putting it mildly," Connor said.

"Were you tempted?" Justin asked, genuinely curious.

Connor shook his head. "No. She has eyes like a dueling gunfighter's."

Justin laughed, spitting a piece of barbecued meat onto the sand. "What do you mean?"

Connor thought for a minute. "I don't really know," he said at last. "Just that she has a look in her eyes, like she'd just as soon kill you as talk to you . . . or kiss you."

"Yeah," Justin said, thinking back to the times he'd been alone with Allegra. "I think I know what you mean, after all."

"Besides, I love Chelsea," Connor said.

"*Besides*?"

Connor looked sheepish. "Well, no, I didn't mean that the way it sounded. I just meant that, well, you never stop noticing other people, other girls."

"You don't?"

"Do you?" Connor asked, gesturing around the lifeguard stand.

"Well . . . no."

"But that doesn't mean you don't love Kate, right? It just means you're not going to ask any of these girls out."

"Of course not," Justin said.

"Well, that's what I meant. I love Chelsea, so I wouldn't go to bed with Allegra if she were the prettiest girl in the world. Which she may be."

"Oh," said Justin.

"But enough of this conversation," Connor said. "See those two little kids building a sand castle? I'll bet you a dollar the one in the red bathing suit starts crying and kicks sand all over the place."

"How can you tell?"

"He has the look."

"Okay, you're on. And if the tides comes in, and they have to start rebuilding, it's double or nothing," Justin said, but his mind was on other things.

Chelsea and Connor met up again and walked home hand in hand.

"So what are you going to do this afternoon?" Connor asked.

"Oh, I thought I'd try to grow a personality," Chelsea said.

"What?" Connor said.

"Nothing," Chelsea said. "Careful, you're about to step on a piece of glass."

She dropped his hand and skipped ahead of him, just out of reach the whole way home.

FOUR

Allegra knocked on the door of the condo. No one answered. She knocked again, louder.

"Okay, okay, hold your horses," she heard Wilton say. He opened the door wearing a towel wrapped around his waist. His hair was dripping wet from the shower.

"Allegra," he said, startled. "How did you find me?"

"I followed you home from the beach, Einstein," Allegra said, pushing past him into the kitchen.

"Look, this isn't a very good time," Wilton said, following her. "I have to be somewhere in, like, five minutes."

"Oh, is tonight your Cub Scout meeting?" Allegra asked sweetly. She took a juice glass out of a cabinet and began opening the other cabinets until she found Wilton's parents' liquor. She poured herself a glass of whiskey, neat.

"Uh, my dad doesn't like people to drink that," Wilton said nervously. "It's quite an expensive bottle from Scotland."

"Well, you'll have to hope he doesn't notice," Allegra said. "Now, where is my coke?"

"It's not here," Wilton said quickly.

"I'll bet."

"It's not. It's in the bank, in a safe-deposit box," Wilton said. "I run one of Grace Caywood's beach stands and I have to take the profits to the bank every single day. It was logical and simple to take the coke with me."

Allegra paused. That did sound plausible. Besides, it was something Chernak might have told him to do. Well, Wilton could just go right back to the bank and get the cocaine out again.

"I've been thinking about our conversation today," she said slowly. "About your notion that we should think up a lie for Chernak."

"Well?" Wilton said. "Did you come up with a better idea?"

"As a matter of fact, I did," Allegra said.

"What?"

"My idea is that you give the coke back to me."

52

"And?"

"And what? That's as much as you need to know."

"Yeah? And what am I supposed to tell Chernak when he sends a couple of goons around to break my kneecaps?" Wilton said sourly.

"Gosh, that's a very good question," Allegra said. "But I'm sure I don't know the answer and I'm not all that interested in sitting around brainstorming with you." She glanced at her watch and her voice brightened. "But I think you can still make it to your safe-deposit box before the bank closes."

Wilton just looked at her.

"Come on," she said. "Quick like a bunny."

Wilton swallowed. "I'm not giving you the coke," he said firmly. "If you don't want to help on this, fine. But I'm not giving you the drugs. Uh-uh. No way."

"Oh, I think you will," Allegra said lightly. She poured herself another tumbler of Wilton's father's Scotch. She sat on a stool and rested her bare feet on the counter. "Because, you see, there's really nothing to stop me from going to Chernak and telling him that you have the coke and that you're thinking about destroying it."

Wilton started to interrupt, but Allegra

held up her hand. "Of course, I know he won't be very pleased to learn that I stole some of his cocaine, but I think he'll get over it. After all, he was once in love with me. But you, well, you're nothing but a liability to him, aren't you?"

Wilton was staring at her, his mouth working silently.

"And think what might happen to your poor brother. What was his name, Eric? Think what might happen to poor Eric if I go to Chernak with that story."

Now Wilton reached for the Scotch. He took a drink straight from the bottle.

"And what happens if I do give you the coke?" he asked at last.

"Why, I'll be gone with the wind," Allegra said. "Never to be seen by you or Chernak again. Don't get me wrong, Wilton. I don't have anything against you. I'm just a girl trying to make a living."

"Oh, sure, you're a real boon to the working classes," Wilton said sarcastically.

Allegra shrugged. "You'd better get a move on," she said. "Time's a-wasting."

"I'm thinking," Wilton said.

"Look, all it takes is a phone call," Allegra said, nodding toward the phone on the kitchen wall.

"Oh, yeah? How do you know where Chernak is, anyway?"

"I don't," Allegra said smoothly. "But I'd guess the Ocean City Grande. And if not, well, I'll just sit down with the yellow pages and call all the hotels in the area. I know every name he uses." She raised her eyebrows. "You want to stand by and watch? Or do you want to go get the coke for me like a good little boy?"

Wilton sighed. He took another drink. "I'll get the coke like a good boy," he said wearily. "Sit tight."

He left the room.

"I thought the coke was at the bank," Allegra called after him.

He didn't answer. A moment later he was back, with four plastic bags in his arms.

"One, two, three, four," he said tonelessly, dropping them into her lap. "Now, please get out of here."

Allegra stood up and stuffed the bags of cocaine into her purse. Wilton walked her to the door. They stood on the terrace for a moment.

"Well, a pleasure doing business with you." Allegra stuck out her hand.

Wilton ignored it and stuffed his hands in his pockets.

"I'm sorry we couldn't get to know each other under—"

"Look," Wilton interrupted. "Would you mind leaving? My parents are going to be home soon."

Allegra threw back her head and laughed. "Oh, my God, that's classic! Your parents are going to be home soon! I feel like I'm doing business with the paper boy!" She went down the stairs, shaking her head and still laughing softly to herself.

Grace looked at the clock. Wilton was fifteen minutes late. Well, that was nothing, right? Except that he lived only *three* minutes away, so he couldn't be stuck in traffic, or unable to get to a phone. Maybe he just had something to do and got held up doing it, Grace tried to rationalize.

She sighed and ran a comb through her hair again. Then she slapped the comb down on the dresser in irritation. Her hair had looked fine twenty minutes ago. Now it just looked more and more disheveled, because she'd combed it four thousand times.

She took a last look in the mirror: white shorts, denim shirt, sneakers. Just right for a picnic. The cooler was all packed and waiting downstairs. She looked at the clock. Wilton was now twenty minutes late.

She prowled around her room some more,

reluctant to go out and face the others. *Hey, weren't you going out?* they would say. *Didn't you have plans? Weren't you supposed to be gone by now?*

Grace stood by her open bedroom window and listened. She could hear Kate and Justin talking softly, lazily, on the porch. Had they positioned themselves there in order to see Wilton arrive? Which door was Wilton going to come to, anyway? She could hear Roan and Bo's voices rise and fall in the kitchen as they rummaged through the fridge for dinner.

"I know, let's make a casserole," Roan said.

"Gross," Bo said. "Besides, it's too hot to heat up the oven."

"But I like casseroles," Roan said. "I find them *comforting.*"

"Okay, the next cold snap, we'll have a casserole," Bo said agreeably. "Tonight let's just have cereal or—Hey, how about these sandwiches?"

"No, those are Grace's," Roan said. "She only spent like a hundred hours making them this afternoon. She's going on a picnic."

Grace rolled her eyes. She had not spent "a hundred hours" making sandwiches, but she had spent a while. She didn't want any two sandwiches to be the same, and she didn't want them to be ordinary, so the cooler was packed with a cream cheese and sliced olive sandwich, a tomato and cucumber sandwich, a cucumber and watercress sandwich, a cream cheese and marmalade sandwich, and an onion and tomato sandwich. There was also a bottle of chilled Perrier and a box of Wilton's favorite cookies.

And now Wilton wasn't even going to show up! Grace looked at the clock again. Thirty-five minutes late. Well, she would just march into the kitchen and tell Bo he could have as many of those sandwiches as he wanted. Besides, what did she care about Wilton the Bookworm? She could go out with guys a hundred times more handsome—

The doorbell rang.

Grace flew down the stairs, through the living room, and down the hall to the front door, in—she would have been surprised to know this—less than eleven seconds. She threw open the front door and stood there, flushed and beautiful, staring at Wilton.

"Hey," he said admiringly. "I thought you were going to be furious because I was so late. But maybe I should be late more often, because you look incredible."

Grace's eyes flashed dangerously.

"Or maybe not," Wilton said hastily. "Look, I'm really sorry, but my parents came home and wanted to talk about a million things."

"It's okay," Grace said icily.

Wilton put his finger under her chin and tilted her face up. "I'm really sorry," he said.

"It's *okay*," she said impatiently.

"Then why are you standing so far away from me?" Wilton asked.

Grace shrugged. Then she smiled, hopped over two steps, and threw her arms around him. Maybe she was happy to see him after all.

Allegra held her purse as though it were her firstborn child. She ate dinner at a diner—an egg salad sandwich, the cheapest thing on the menu. She had to make the money Grace gave her last until she could sell the cocaine. But her spirits were high. *Not for long*, she thought joyfully. *Not many more egg salad sandwiches to go.*

She kept her purse on her lap all through dinner, the strap wrapped around her ankle. It would be just her luck to have some idiot snatch her purse tonight of all nights.

After dinner Allegra walked slowly back to the Seaside. The motel was even more depressing, if that was possible, in the soft light of evening. The ancient aqua paint was chipping off to reveal even-more-ancient pink paint beneath it. The screen doors sagged on rusty hinges, and crabgrass poked through cracks in the sidewalk.

Allegra thought it looked like a bad painting—though not as bad as the painting of a clown that hung over the bed in her room, room six. She thought that if an artist painted a picture of the Seaside, people who saw it later would think that the artist had added all sorts of squalid details—the overflowing Dumpster, somebody's abandoned red tennis shoe, the two old men eating doughnuts on the front stoop, Allegra's guitar-playing neighbor singing "My Old Kentucky Home." But the sad part was that all the details were real. Allegra tried to think of a catchy title for this painting. *The Last-Stop Motel*? *The No-Hope Hotel*?

She stopped walking halfway through the parking lot, clutching her purse to her chest. What was she going to do—take her beloved stash, her most precious possession, into that dump? Oh, no. No, sir. Even if she stayed awake all night guarding it, it wouldn't be safe in the Seaside, where the rooms were probably habitually robbed.

Allegra turned and began walking rapidly

in the opposite direction. What had she been thinking? And anyway, if Chernak decided to pay her a friendly—or not-so-friendly—little visit, she didn't want the coke right there on the premises. That was something Wilton would do.

Allegra thought about Wilton for a second. He'd been rattled, but still a lot cooler than she ever imagined. In fact, she'd believed him when he said the drugs were in a safe-deposit box. She remembered him saying, *I run one of Grace Caywood's beach stands, and I have to take the profits to the bank every single day.* Grace Caywood? Was that her Grace, Allegra's Grace?

Why, I'm sounding possessive, Allegra thought with surprise. *I'm acting like she's my best friend or something.*

Of course, Grace was the closest thing Allegra had to a friend, best or otherwise. So maybe Grace hadn't been slopping over with sugar when she'd helped Allegra out, but still, she *had* helped, and Allegra was grateful.

I wonder if it is the same Grace, she thought. *And Wilton's one of her employees? I wonder if he has a gigantic crush on her?*

She stopped, realizing that she had automatically walked back to the beach. She still hadn't thought of a safe place to hide the bricks of cocaine. She glanced at her watch. The banks were closed. Too bad. Otherwise she could have used Wilton's idea of a safe-deposit box.

Should she try to talk her way into Grace's house and then hide the coke there? No one would ever suspect any of the goody-goodies in that house of possession. Although who would have suspected *Wilton?* Okay, so say she stashed the coke in Grace's house. . . . There were, what—five or six people living there? What if some chucklehead found it? She could just picture the scene: *Hey, everyone, look what I found! Powdered sugar! Let's make frosting!* Or what if she couldn't talk her way back in to get it? No, Allegra decided regretfully, Grace's house was too risky.

So where did that leave her? Allegra strolled along the beach, deep in thought. She passed one of Grace's beach stands and stopped. She turned and looked at it. She could bury the coke in the sand, just like she'd done on the island. She'd been able to sit literally on top of it all day. What could be safer? Of course, with her luck, some little kid would try to dig a hole to China right there, but . . . It seemed like her best bet. No place was going to be completely safe.

It took Allegra nearly forty minutes to dig a hole deep enough. Two feet, she judged. Well, that ought to be good enough. Tenderly she placed the plump white plastic bricks in the hole and scraped sand back over them. *Good night*, she said to them silently. *Hopefully, you won't have to stay there very long. Hopefully, I'll have a buyer in a day or so.*

Allegra stood up and stretched. Her back ached and her fingernails were broken and grimy, but she felt terrific. Her future was secure again.

She began walking back to the Seaside with a spring in her step. Halfway there she broke out in song—"My Old Kentucky Home."

FIVE

Connor sighed, stretched, and turned off his computer. He glanced at his watch. Seven fifteen. He frowned. He had asked Chelsea to knock on the door at seven, so they could make plans for dinner.

He stood up and stretched again. He'd written nearly twelve pages this afternoon. The book was beginning to pick up speed.

Connor went into the bedroom. Chelsea was lying on her stomach on the bed in her bathrobe, reading a magazine. Her shower-damp hair hung down her back in a mass of curls. She flipped the pages of the magazine in an almost angry, absent-minded way: *snap*, pause, *snap*, pause.

"Hey, Chels," he said softly, lying down next to her. "I thought you were going to interrupt me at seven."

"I didn't want to interrupt you while you were working so hard," Chelsea said without looking up. *Snap*, went a page of the magazine. Chelsea's foot beat absently on the bedspread.

"Well, I wasn't working *that* hard," Connor said. "So, anyway, what do you want to do for dinner?"

"I don't know," Chelsea said. She turned the last page of the magazine, flipped it over, and started again. *Snap, snap, snap.* "Maybe I shouldn't eat dinner. If I gained weight, you might not like me anymore."

Connor laughed. "Chels, that's crazy."

Chelsea looked at him out of the corner of her eye. "Oh, that's right, you don't like my body, you love my mind."

A faint alarm bell sounded in Connor's head. "I like both," he said cautiously.

Chelsea turned on her side to face him. "But which do you like *better*, Connor?"

"Well, I don't really think of it that way," Connor said slowly. He sensed a trap, but didn't know what to look out for. "It's not like I think of your body versus your mind. I like the whole package. I—"

"*Package*?"

Connor winced. "Well, maybe not package, but—"

"But why do you *love* me? Why did you *marry* me?" Chelsea asked. She snuggled closer and put her hand on his chest. "Was it for my integrity, my sense of humor, my intellect, my sterling *mind*?"

Connor knew there was a right and a wrong answer. But he didn't know what Chelsea was paving the way for. "What are you getting at?" he asked. "Why all these questions?'

"I'm just curious," Chelsea said. She kissed his collarbone. She was nearly purring. "What's the matter? Why don't you answer me? Did you marry me for my mind or my body? It's a very simple question."

The phone rang.

Saved by the bell, Connor thought joyfully, but Chelsea pressed him back onto the bed. "Let the machine get it," she said.

"Why?"

"Because we're talking."

"Uh-huh. But it might be Justin or Kate or somebody."

"Well, if it's Jason or Kara, you can call them back."

"Sure, but I might as well just answer the—" Connor stopped. He stared at Chelsea. She tucked a stray lock of hair behind her ear and smiled at him sweetly.

There was a very long silence.

Connor went from lying down to standing up in one fluid motion. He looked like a cartoon, and Chelsea wanted to laugh. "You've been readin' me book!" Connor shouted. His Irish brogue thickened when he was angry. "Oh, Lord almighty! You've been readin' it, haven't you!"

"Connor, I just—"

"Snoopin'!" Connor yelled. "Snoopin' through my things! So that's why all these questions about do I like your mind, or do I like your body! Jesus, Mary, and Joseph!"

"I wasn't snooping," Chelsea said hotly. "It was sitting right there on the nightstand. It might have been someone else's manuscript from your writers' group for all I knew. I thought I would just read a page or two—"

"Someone else's manuscript? Good heavens above, girl. Don't give me that. You knew perfectly well what it was."

"Okay, so maybe I did." Chelsea stood up on the bed. Even so, she was still shorter than Connor. "But there's no reason for *you* to fly off the handle. How do you think *I* feel?" She suddenly imitated Connor's accent. "Charisse was a sweet lass, but who really cared? She had a great—"

"Chelsea!"

"Well, it's true!"

Connor swallowed. "Sweetheart," he began again, struggling to keep his voice steady. "You shouldn't have read it without my permission."

"*Forget that!*" Chelsea howled. "Tell me once and for all whether you married me for my body or my mind?"

"Chelsea, that's ridiculous. You're hoping that I'll say I married you for your body, so you can be furious. But if I say I married you for your mind, you'll be furious and say that I don't think you're pretty."

Suddenly Chelsea laughed. "That's true," she said. "You can't win this one, sluggo."

"So let me off the hook then," Connor said. He stepped nearer the bed and pulled Chelsea toward him by the belt of her robe. "When you read the rest of the book, you'll see that I worship your body and respect your mind."

"Well, I'm already on page two hundred, and I don't see that yet," Chelsea said.

"Page two hundred!" Connor said. "You've read that much in one day?"

"Yeah," Chelsea said absently. "I got caught up."

Connor put his arms around her waist. "Well?"

"Well, what?"

"You said you got caught up. So it's compelling, right?"

"Oh, good Lord, now you're fishing for compliments!" She wrinkled her nose at him, but her arms crept around his neck.

"Well . . . do you have any compliments to give?"

Chelsea thought for a moment. "I thought it was funny, well paced, and a little bit like *Catcher in the Rye*," she said. "Plus, I think you made some things up."

"It's a *novel*," Connor said. "I made it *all* up."

Allegra took a long shower in her motel room. The showers at the Seaside Motel sputtered and gusted and changed from hot to cold without warning, but Allegra didn't mind. Not tonight. Things were finally going her way again.

She dressed in a pair of denim shorts and a pink halter top. She brushed her heavy auburn hair straight back from her forehead, knowing that as it dried it would fall forward to gently frame her face. She didn't bother with any makeup. She left the Seaside humming, her sandals flapping against the gravel of the parking lot.

69

She walked back to the boardwalk. *My legs are going to be in great shape*, she thought. *The secret is simple: no money for a car or food.*

She perched on a section of railing not cluttered with kissing couples or touristy-looking older people. The sun was setting behind her. Allegra thought briefly how pretty her hair must look in the reflection of the sunset, but then she shrugged. She had more important things to worry about than attracting men. She pulled a beat-up paperback book out of her back pocket. It was titled *Doctors and Nurses*, and Allegra had picked it up in the Seaside's office. She pretended to read it while she scanned the people on the boardwalk. She knew that she would find what she wanted sooner or later.

She saw signs of what she was looking for right away: The first possibility was a blond girl wearing a lot of black eyeliner who walked with a staggering, burned-out gait, but whose eyes were as sharp and alert as a hawk's. Then there were the groups of nervous-looking teenagers, hanging together and whispering, constantly pooling their money and saying, "You carry it." "No, *you* carry it."

Next she watched a young boy of about twelve who tore up and down the boardwalk on a skateboard. He never smiled or laughed, and Allegra noticed that he checked one of the railing posts as he sped by it. What was he looking for? she wondered. Whatever it was, he evidently hadn't seen it because he didn't stop. He was off down the boardwalk, out of sight, and she would have to wait for him to return again.

Allegra actually felt a small flicker of hope when she noticed a woman of forty wearing tennis whites suddenly stop by one of the railing posts and get down on her hands and knees. Was that the sign? Should Allegra do that? But then a man walking next to the woman said, "For heaven's sake, Muriel, what are you doing?" and Muriel said, "I'm looking for my contact lens! Get down here and help me!" The search seemed so futile that Allegra finally had to get down and help them; she felt like a heel just sitting there watching. Muriel let out a small cry of joy when she finally saw the contact lens glimmering in a pile of sand. She and her husband moved off down the boardwalk.

Allegra knew that she was getting closer to what she was looking for as more people began lingering pointedly around that particular post. She leaned against the railing and pretended to be engrossed in her paperback.

A girl in a red letter jacket put a Coke can on the railing near the post. Milling around were a bald man in an old-fashioned T-strap undershirt, the eyeliner girl, and two young boys with a portable radio. If Allegra had been asked *how* she knew what these people were after, she wouldn't have been able to answer, because they didn't really look different from other people on the boardwalk. It was just something Allegra sensed—or recognized—from her exposure to people involved with drugs.

The crowd around the post scattered whenever the skateboard boy approached, and then regrouped, sullenly, looking resentful. Allegra wondered how many times the skateboard boy would pass them before he deemed it safe enough to stop.

He skated by four times. Well, maybe it was five. Allegra actually got caught up in one of the steamier parts of *Doctors and Nurses* and lost count. But finally there he was, pulling the bald man aside first. Allegra glimpsed a money belt around the boy's waist when his rugby shirt rode up a little. She smiled.

One by one, with many pauses for skateboarding, the boy seemed to take care of everyone, and in a way so quick and so smooth that even Allegra had trouble spotting the transactions. The briefest touch of fingers, a hand in a pocket, a nod, and it was over. She was impressed.

When the last of the crowd dispersed, the skateboard boy took off down the boardwalk. Allegra retrieved the Coke can out of the trash where the bald man had dumped it and put it back in its place on the railing. Then she leaned against the post until the skateboard boy came back into view. To her surprise, he stopped immediately.

"Hello, pretty lady," he said.

"Hello." She paused, smiled. "I've been waiting for you."

"Just name the place, beautiful," the boy said.

"*You're twelve years old.*"

"Thirteen. And a half."

"Great. Look, I really have been waiting for you. I need—"

"Well, sorry to disappoint you, sweetie-pie, but I'm just a kid on a board, you know? I can't help you with whatever you need." The kid turned a lazy circle on the board.

Allegra continued as though he hadn't spoken. "I need you to tell your boss that I have a package for him. A very big package, if he can afford to buy it."

73

The boy was making wider circles, ignoring her. "Look, lady, I don't have a boss, I don't know anything about packages, I'm just—"

"I'll bring a sample here tomorrow night, same time."

The skateboard thudded against the wooden planks of the boardwalk. "How many times do I have to tell you, I'm—"

"Just a kid on a board, I know," Allegra said. She turned and walked away. The kid would tell his boss. If not tonight, then tomorrow, after he tested the sample. And sooner or later this information would work its way up the drug food-chain until Allegra had a buyer. *Or until Chernak hears about it*, she thought with a shiver of fear.

She met Muriel and her husband walking the other way. "Oh, hello," Allegra said. "Did you get your contact lens back in?"

"Oh, yes," Muriel said. "I put it in when we got to our friend's house."

"You should see Muriel put in her contacts," Muriel's husband said to Allegra. "She can throw them up in the air and catch them in her eyes, practically. She's been wearing them for years."

"Well, good night," Allegra said.

"Good night, dear," Muriel said. "And

thanks again for helping us. It's so rare to find a lovely young woman like you these days. So many young people are terribly callous."

Grace tasted the whiskey on Wilton's breath the minute he kissed her. She pulled away, surprised. "Have you been drinking?" she asked.

Wilton lay back on the blanket. The remains of their picnic were scattered around them. "You could taste it?" he asked. "Even after I ate five sandwiches?"

Grace nodded. "I know some alcoholics who use vanilla extract in place of perfume because the alcohol content in perfume is too high for them. I used to live for booze. I can sense it a mile away." She leaned over and kissed him. "Or five sandwiches away."

"I'm sorry," Wilton said.

"Don't be. I don't care if you drink—you can even drink in front of me," Grace said. "It just surprised me that you would have a drink before you came to pick me up." She hesitated. "Are you—nervous or unsure about going out with me?"

"Are you kidding?" Wilton said. "I've only wanted to go out with you from the first second I met you."

But Grace was still serious. "I'm only asking

because you seem a little preoccupied. You've been staring at the boardwalk all evening."

Wilton looked over at the boardwalk. "Yeah, well, I thought I saw Allegra go by."

"You know Allegra?"

"We met on the beach," Wilton said vaguely. "Boy, she gives me the willies."

"In what way?"

"Never mind," he said, turning back to her. He traced a finger along one of her eyebrows. "What were we talking about? You were saying you think I don't want to go out with you or something?"

Grace suddenly felt foolish. "I don't know. . . . Forget I brought it up."

"No, let's talk about it," Wilton said. He smiled. "Go ahead, ask me anything."

"Anything? Okay, what's the square root of 445?"

Wilton rolled his eyes, and Grace thought for one horrible moment that he would rattle off the answer. But he said, "No, I mean ask me something personal. We can play *High-Q* later, if you want to."

"Okay . . . well, tell me about your former girlfriends."

"Oh, that's an easy one. I don't have any. Next question."

"What do you mean, you don't have any former girlfriends!" Grace said.

"I mean, I never went out with anyone. What do you think I mean?"

"No one? Ever?"

"Gee, you're really making me feel good about myself."

"I'm sorry," Grace said contritely. She snuggled closer to him and kissed his cheek. "I just find it hard to believe that no one but me has ever fallen for your charms."

Wilton rested his arm around her shoulders. "Well, how do you think I feel? I still can't believe you chose me over Carr."

"Oh, Wilton, you don't have to be jealous of Carr! He's in Kansas anyway."

Wilton laughed. "Boy, that makes me feel just great. I don't have to worry because Carr's almost halfway across the country. But if he were still here, I guess I'd be out of luck."

"That's not what I meant!" Grace said, laughing. "I'm sorry, Wilton." She kissed him. "You don't have to worry, period. Now, come on, you must've had a girlfriend or two in there somewhere."

Wilton shrugged. "I always had a lot of girls as friends. And I liked some of them as more than friends."

"Well, didn't anyone you were friends with like *you* as more than friends?"

"Oh, yeah, this one girl," Wilton said. "Her name was Mary Louise Hamburg, and she was the smartest girl in the whole school and she asked me to do a science fair project with her."

"And what happened?"

"Well, okay, for months we worked in the school basement, teaching this pigeon to walk a maze. I mean, Mary Louise insisted that we go there every single *night*, and sometimes she looked at me a little mistily, but I didn't really think anything of it."

"And?" Grace prompted, surprised to find herself caring.

"So, anyway, we won second place at the science fair, and afterward I went up to Mary Louise and shook hands with her and said it was great working together, and she said, 'Is that it? Is that all you have to say to me?' "

"Oh, no."

"Oh, yes. I didn't know what she was talking about, and I thought maybe she thought she'd done more work on the project than me and was waiting for me to say congratulations, so I did."

"Wilton! Did she start crying and run into the bathroom?"

"No . . . she stomped off and refused to shake hands with the principal and everything. Later she called my parents' answering machine and left a message saying that I was a really horrible person and that she should have chosen Jay Paterson to be her partner because he was a lot smarter than me and then she would have won first prize instead of lousy second place."

Grace lay back on the blanket, choking with laughter. "Don't you have any *good* stories?" she asked at last. "Didn't you ever go to the prom or anything?"

Wilton's face lit up. "You want to hear my prom story?"

"Dear God, I don't think so," Grace said hastily. "Let's play that *High-Q* game now."

"Okay," Wilton said agreeably.

"All right . . ." Grace glanced up at the sky. "How did the constellations get their names?"

Wilton lay down next to her and held her hand. As he answered her question in long and staggering detail, Grace watched his face and thought she must be going crazy to like him so much.

SIX

Kate sat on her lifeguard stand. Her bright blue eyes swept the ocean: two little kids swimming deeper than they should. But okay, they were turning around. A man in goggles was out past the crowd, swimming back and forth, back and forth, getting in shape for some swimming competition, Kate guessed. Well, judging by the strength of his swimming, he certainly could take care of himself. He'd probably outdistance her if she tried to save him. Farther out beyond him, two Jet Skis bobbed brightly up and down, the noise of their engines silent at this distance. And there was a slender, golden-bronzed girl in an orange bikini asking Justin for something—

Wait a minute! Kate told herself. *You're*

supposed to be watching the ocean. But she focused her gaze on Justin a moment longer. He was lifting his first-aid kit out from under his seat. He handed the girl an item from the kit. Kate resisted the impulse to use her binoculars to see exactly what it was. Probably a Band-Aid, she thought. The girl lingered, said something. Justin smiled, his white teeth gleaming for an instant, but then he put his own binoculars up to his eyes and looked out at the swimmers. The girl waited patiently, but he didn't stop looking out at the ocean, and after a moment she shrugged slightly and went back to her blanket.

Well, if you're through checking up on your boyfriend, maybe you could get back to work, a voice in Kate's mind spoke up.

Okay, okay. She checked her area again. The two little kids were back in the shallow area, the goggle-man was swimming like a fish (we should *hire* him, Kate thought), and the two Jet Skis were still tearing around, but they were heading into Justin's area. Good, let him worry about them.

She sat back in her chair. Her eyes still flickered automatically over the crowd, but her mind was elsewhere. She thought about her conversation with Chelsea. *Is it hard to be in love with someone who attracts so many girls?*

Kate sighed. Of course it was hard . . . but she'd meant what she'd said about not being able to imagine herself or Justin with anyone else. But if they were never going to be with anyone else, where did that leave them?

She rolled her eyes. She didn't really think of either one of them as marriage material—at least, not yet. *Well, do you have to make all your life decisions today?* the voice inside her head asked.

No, of course she didn't. She had other things to do. Her job, for one. Kate lifted her binoculars to her eyes.

Justin squinted at the Jet Skiers until his eyes hurt. Neither he nor Kate wore sunglasses on the job—the chances were too great that you could miss something. The Jet Skiers were doing some fancy spins now. Great, Justin thought, blowing out his breath in aggravation. As if it weren't enough that they were going way too fast. He wanted to blow his whistle and warn them, but they would never hear it. He could barely hear *them*, the engines making only a faint *zip, zip* sound.

The Jet Skis had come from Kate's area. Justin glanced over at her stand and saw that her eyes were on them, too.

He watched Kate, thinking about the night before. They had sat on the deck talking about nothing in particular, watched Grace leave with some studious-looking person in glasses, made dinner, gone to bed. It was wonderful. It was the first time in their relationship that they weren't under all kinds of stress, and Justin loved it. He loved the day-to-dayness of it, the routine, and this surprised him. He thought of Connor yesterday, hinting that he and Kate were ready to get married. Justin snorted. Hardly. Kate only had a million plans for the future, and he had some of his own, too. Still . . . didn't Kate figure into those plans? He couldn't imagine anything without—

Sudden movement on the water caught his eyes. The Jet Skiers were now racing each other, running some sort of slalom. Justin jumped to his feet. The Jet Skis bumped each other and spun, but after a moment they were back on their slalom course. Justin was furious. Were they crazy? They would kill themselves.

His eyes searched the horizon for the Beach Patrol boat. He spotted it way down by the inlet. Justin was reaching for his flags when he noticed that Kate was ahead of him, already semaphoring to the patrol boat.

Good move, Kate, he thought, but he knew the boat was too far away to see the signal.

Justin blew his whistle to clear the water, and a moment later he heard Kate do the same. The Beach Patrol boat was turning around. So slow, so slow.

Justin met Kate's eyes, and he signaled to her. They hit the sand running for the water.

Allegra heard Kate and Justin blowing their whistles to clear the water, and she thought, *Oh, great, what's the problem? A shark?*

She was staring at the note a man in a black leather jacket had handed her: *Meet me at the snack bar as soon as you can.*

She glanced up and saw Justin and Kate swimming toward two daredevil Jet Skiers. Allegra shrugged. Who cared if the Jet Skiers killed themselves?

A crowd was gathering, standing on the beach and craning their necks to see what the commotion was all about. *Okay, this is great,* she thought. *Everyone on the beach will be distracted while I'm ironing out the last few details of the drug deal.*

She pulled a baseball cap on over her auburn hair, slid on a pair of sunglasses, and walked to the snack bar.

Black Leather Jacket was eating a hot dog at the condiment stand.

She walked up and tapped him on the shoulder. He jumped about a foot. "What do you think you're doing?" he said around a mouthful of hot dog.

"Oh, I'm sorry," Allegra said mockingly. In loud pig latin she said, "Ug-dray eal-day?"

"Shut *up*," Leather Jacket said. He grabbed her by the arm and pulled her over against a wall of the snack bar. "Will you shut up and not attract so much attention?"

"Look, you're the one who wore a leather jacket to the *beach*," Allegra said, not at all bothered. "Now, as I told that kid last night, I'll be on the boardwalk at ten o'clock—"

"Wait a minute," Leather Jacket said. "First of all, we want to know—"

"*With* a sample, as I said," Allegra continued. "I assume you have a tester. If you like the sample, there's a lot more where it came from. My price is a quarter million in cash. I don't think we have anything more to say to each other. If you're not there tonight, I'll assume you couldn't raise the money."

Leather Jacket was fuming. "Listen, princess, *we* choose the meeting place. We'll send a car for you tonight—" He broke off when he saw Allegra shaking her head.

"Thanks, but I don't particularly want a one-way car ride to the Ocean City dump, or wherever you plan to leave me."

"Well, the boardwalk is out of the question. It's crawling with cops," Leather Jacket said.

She looked at him, narrowing her green eyes. "I haven't noticed any, but I'll tell you what," she said softly. "We'll do it right here, tomorrow. Plenty of witnesses for me, no cops for you."

"How the hell—"

Allegra pointed at a nearby family's blue-and-white cooler. "Buy a cooler just like that one and put a tester and the cash in it," she said. "Set up a chaise lounge near my blanket. I'll give you a sample, you test it, and if it meets your high standards"—she smiled—"then I'll give you an identical cooler with the drugs in it. You give me the cooler with the cash. No one will suspect a thing."

My, but Chernak would be proud of her. She was acting like a professional, thinking on her feet. She smiled again.

Leather Jacket was mulling it over. Finally he nodded. "Okay," he said.

Allegra was a little suspicious about his quick agreement, but she struggled to keep the upper hand. "Good," she said shortly.

"Wear a bathing suit instead of your jacket and maybe carry a magazine or something."

Leather Jacket smiled at her sourly.

"And remember, we're going to be on my turf, at high noon, in front of a million people, so don't try anything."

Leather Jacket took off his sunglasses, and Allegra realized he was probably only about eighteen or so. "High noon?" he said. "I'm supposed to meet you at *high noon*?"

"That's what I said, isn't it?"

"Well, what time is high noon?"

"Twelve o'clock."

"So why not just say *noon*?" Leather Jacket asked.

"Okay, *one* o'clock," Allegra snapped, losing her temper. "Just bring the money, and I don't care what time you show up."

She turned and flounced angrily back to her blanket, her long fiery hair swaying and her feet kicking up little sprays of sand.

The Jet Skis collided before Justin and Kate reached them. Justin heard the noise of the crash, which was a surprisingly dull *thud*, not like the screech and crunch of a car accident. He slowed his strokes as his heart contracted for a moment; then he doubled his speed.

Both Jet Skis had left the collision rider-less. As Justin found the first body floating in the water, he saw one of the Jet Skis do a slow dipsy-doodle and heard its engine stall. The other Jet Ski roared around them in a circle.

"Kate!" Justin called, but she headed past him. *She must see the other rider somewhere in the water,* he thought.

Justin turned his attention to the boy in his arms. He was out cold, with an ugly red gash on his forehead. Justin pried the boy's eyes open while trying to tread water. He couldn't hold still enough in the choppy ocean to see the boy's pupils, but the eyes weren't filling with blood.

"Keep breathing, kid . . . keep breathing," Justin said. He tucked the boy's head in the crook of his arm and looked around for Kate, to tell her he was heading back for shore.

Kate was struggling with the other rider, a boy of about fifteen. He was screaming because of the blood in his eyes, and she was trying to calm him down.

"Kate!" Justin called. Maybe he should hand her the unconscious kid and take the other one? He was stronger, but Kate knew what she was doing.

"Kate?" he called again, but she ignored him. She was trying to get near the bleeding boy, who was thrashing so wildly that Justin knew he'd tire out in a minute or—

"*Kate*! *Look out*!" Justin screamed, and the urgency in his voice made Kate look up. She looked at him, and he could see the puzzlement in her eyes.

The growl of the second riderless Jet Ski had become white noise to them both, and Kate never even heard it as it roared up behind her. It swerved suddenly and Justin thought it would be okay, but then the Jet Ski veered the other way and slammed into the back of Kate's head in a wave of white foam.

Grace trudged slowly through the sand toward Wilton's beach stand. She was so preoccupied with thoughts about Wilton that she didn't hear or notice any of the commotion farther down the beach. She couldn't shake the feeling that something was bothering Wilton—he acted so distant when they were together . . . when they were talking . . . even when they were kissing.

So now she going to visit him at work with a thermos of lemonade, and she felt lousy about it. She felt like she was chasing him, crowding him. What if Wilton looked up and saw her and thought, *Oh, no, here she comes?*

Grace stood up a little straighter. Why

was she acting like this? She *never* acted like this. She didn't like tricks and scheming. She would just be herself, and Wilton could take her or leave her.

"Hello, Wilton," she said briskly, marching up to his stand.

Wilton was staring off into space, but when he heard her voice, he looked up and beamed. *His face lights up*, Grace thought in puzzlement. *I can actually make this person's face light up, and yet he'd rather be boiled in oil than tell me what he's thinking.*

"I brought you some lemonade," she said, setting the thermos in front of him.

"Oh, that's great!" Wilton said. He poured some lemonade into the cap of the thermos. "I hate the stuff in cans."

"I thought you would."

"Why?" Wilton looked up from his drink. The foam of the lemonade had left a slight mustache on his upper lip.

Grace smiled. "Well, you just seem like an old-fashioned kind of guy. . . . Hey, you're not reading anything today?"

"No, not in the mood," Wilton said.

Grace looked at him. This from the guy who carried a book with him to the movies so that he didn't have to waste ten minutes waiting for the film to start?

"Wilton," she began, and paused.

"Hmm?" Wilton was staring off into space again. No, not space, she realized. He was staring off toward Allegra, who was camped out on a blanket a short distance away.

Grace could see Allegra's auburn hair and her perfect profile, but she shrugged. Grace was not capable of jealousy; it was simply not within her range of emotions. She was too happy with herself. She wondered if Wilton had some problem with Allegra, some awkward run-in. She couldn't imagine how or why, though.

"Wilton, I have to ask you some—" she began again, but her words were drowned out by the sudden shouting of the crowd gathered at the water's edge.

Grace and Wilton both looked down the beach to see what was happening, but their view of the ocean was blocked.

"What were you saying?" Wilton asked.

Grace shook her head absently, still staring down the beach.

"Hey," Wilton said softly. "Whatever the emergency is, they'll take care of it. They're trained to do that." He took her hand. "What were you going to ask me?"

Grace looked at him. He still had a slight lemonade mustache. She smiled, and wiped it off gently with her fingertip. "I was . . ." She paused and tilted her head, as though listening for something. Foreboding, and a strange sense of urgency, filled her. She turned and looked at the ocean once more. She couldn't see Kate and Justin—she was too far away.

She took a few hesitant steps.

"Grace?"

She didn't turn around, she barely heard him. Suddenly it was an effort to hear anything through the pulsing pressure in her mind. "I'll talk to you later," she said vaguely, and began walking rapidly down the beach. She broke into a run a few minutes later, and soon she was sprinting, her long legs pumping, her lungs feeling ready to burst.

The noise of the Jet Ski hitting Kate was worse than Justin could ever have imagined. It sounded like a cantaloupe being split open. For the rest of his life, at unexpected moments—while helping a child tie her shoelace, while trying to remember where he left his keys, just before he fell asleep—Justin would think he heard that sound again.

It happened so fast, he could barely believe it. The Jet Ski hit Kate, flipped, and sank, its engine still gunning, creating its own minor whirlpool. The bleeding boy, who hadn't stopped screaming, now doubled his efforts. Waves from the Jet Ski washed over Justin, blinding him while he tried to find Kate.

He was furious with helplessness. He tried to see in the churning saltwater. He tried to hang on to the unconscious boy in his arms. Could he let go? Where was Kate? *Where was Kate?*

Kate, hold on, I'm coming, I'll be there . . .

Now the screaming, bleeding boy was going under. A wave tossed him into Justin, and he threw his arms around Justin with the strength of the drowning. Justin's head snapped backward, and his mouth and lungs filled with water. He thrashed uncontrollably, letting go of the unconscious boy, trying to loosen the arms of the bleeding one. All the while his mind clamored for Kate.

And suddenly—suddenly, there were other people in the water with him. Strong, capable people. A girl in a life vest put her arms around him. "Sir?" she questioned. "Sir—"

Justin coughed up seawater. He struggled in the girl's grip. "My girlfriend—" he gasped. "Hit—in the head—"

"She's already on board, sir," the girl said. Justin saw the Beach Patrol boat bobbing behind her.

Thank God.

"Others—"

"We got them, too," the girl said. "Two boys and a girl. Is that everyone?"

Justin nodded.

"Then will you please come with me, sir?"

Justin realized he was still struggling. He stopped, and let the girl pull him toward the boat. A dozen strong hands reached down to pull him aboard.

He landed on deck and coughed up the last of the seawater. His throat was raw. He looked around for Kate as the boat picked up speed.

He saw her lying a few feet away, covered with a blanket. A Beach Patrol guard was performing mouth-to-mouth.

Justin tapped him on the shoulder. "Let me," he said.

"Back off," the guy said without missing a breath.

Justin swallowed. "Please," he said. "It's okay. I'm a lifeguard and she's my girlfriend."

The guy shrugged, then held up four fingers. Breath, three fingers, breath, two fingers, breath, one finger, breath—

And Justin covered Kate's mouth with his own. He steadied her head with his hand. His fingers froze. Was that a *dent*? *Oh, my God— did Kate have a dent in her skull?*

Justin blew air into Kate's lungs, listened, blew again. He had barely gotten his own wind back, but he didn't notice. His tender throat burned, but he paid no attention, forcing air into Kate faster and faster as they headed for shore.

SEVEN

Grace elbowed her way viciously through the crowd at the water's edge in time to watch Justin and two Beach Patrol guards lifting Kate out of the white motorboat. Other Beach Patrol guards followed, carrying two teenaged boys. The crowd parted obediently to let them through to the waiting ambulances.

Grace turned and tried to make her way to the ambulances, but the crowd had neither forgotten nor forgiven her ruthlessness in getting to the front. By the time she squeaked through, the ambulances were already driving away.

Grace stopped and took a breath. Her heart was hammering. Okay, well, no big mystery where the ambulances were going—

there was only one hospital in Ocean City. Now she just had to get there. She ran back to Wilton's beach stand.

"Are you okay?" he asked, frowning at her pale face. "*Three* ambulances—what was that all about?"

"I don't know yet," Grace said. "But I need you to close the stand."

"Close the stand—"

"I'm your boss, Wilton! If I say close the stand, you close the stand!" Grace's voice wavered, and she tried to control it. "Kate and Justin were hurt—I have to get to the hospital."

Wilton was already in motion, pulling down the metal bars that protected the stand at night.

"I need you to call Bo and Roan for me and tell them there's been an accident—or something," Grace continued. If only she could keep her voice businesslike. It wasn't working.

Wilton locked up the stand and put his arms around her. She rested her head against his shoulder and said, "And then I need you to drive me to the hospital and stay there with me, because I really don't think I can do this by myself."

● ● ●

Justin sat beside Kate in the ambulance, refusing to let go of her hand and driving the paramedics crazy. The mouth-to-mouth had worked to start her breathing again, but she hadn't opened her eyes.

"Is she in a coma or just unconscious?"

"I don't know," one paramedic said. He was a big beefy guy.

"You don't know?" Justin repeated.

"No, I don't know," the beefy guy said. "Because you won't even let go of her hand long enough for me to get her pulse, let alone anything else."

"Well, she has two hands—" Justin began.

"Look, out of my way, pal," the beefy guy said. The ambulance took a corner fast, throwing them both a little off balance. "Now, I'm going to do what I can to help your girlfriend, but I can't do it with you standing in between us and jabbering a blue streak, so *out of my way!*"

Justin retreated to the far corner of the ambulance and watched the paramedic's huge hands feel for Kate's pulse, lift her eyelids, take her blood pressure.

The paramedic shouted something up to the driver, who grabbed the radio and barked into it. Justin didn't catch most of it because it was in radio jargon, but he heard the word coma and that was enough.

•   •   •

Kate's first thought was: *Hey, there's Mr. Barker.* Mr. Barker was the football coach at her old high school.

But why was Mr. Barker shining a light in her eyes—

That hurts, Kate said.

—and why was the room careening around like this? And did she hear sirens? Why was Mr. Barker wearing a white coat? Where was his beloved Dartmouth football jersey, the one he wore in the game where he first developed the Barker Formation, or whatever he called it? And why was he shining that light in her eyes?

I said that hurts, Kate said again.

There, he finally clicked off the light and let her eyelids close. Kate relaxed into the darkness. Funny, she hadn't heard her own voice. . . . She thought she could taste saltwater. Startled, she opened her eyes. No, it was still dark, so maybe she hadn't opened her eyes. Had someone been drowning? She thought so; she thought it might have been someone close to her. . . .

She felt the huge crowd pressing in at the water's edge. "What happened? Do you think anyone's still alive? Where did that lifeguard go?" Justin, they meant Justin.

There was the Beach Patrol boat at last. "They don't know where to look!" someone cried. People were shouting and waving, trying to direct the rescue boat.

But I'm right here. No, they're not looking for me, they're looking for Justin. . . .

"They're pulling someone out of the water," Chelsea said in her ear. *Where did Chelsea come from? Never mind. Where was Justin? They were pulling someone out, but not Justin, someone else, an older guy.*

Where is he? I love him so much, he can't—

There he was! There was Justin, just a limp figure in red swimming trunks, but at least she could see him, and—and he was waving. Not much but a little. Kate let herself relax. She didn't remember running to him. She just remembered holding him tight and vowing never to let him go.

Kate frowned. Why was she thinking about that accident? That was so long ago. Justin was fine . . . wasn't he? But then where was he? She could remember a commotion on the beach. Had that been about Justin? Was he in danger again? She had to get up, go to him. But she was so tired and it was so dark. . . . At least the room had stopped spinning.

"Hey, fella," she heard Mr. Barker say. He sounded a mile away, and getting fainter. "Hey, guy, stop crying. We're at the hospital. She's in good hands now. Stop crying, please."

Chelsea and Connor were lying on their bed, eating a bowl of Fritos and paging through Connor's manuscript.

"Now, for instance," Chelsea said with her mouth full, "I never said, 'Oh, Grandma, everyone has sex these days.' And I never *would* say it. Do you know why? Because it would give my poor grandmother a heart attack."

"Chels, I made it *up*—"

"In fact," Chelsea said, sitting up. "Once when our cat had kittens, I said something like, 'What sex are the kittens?' and my grandmother got this really shocked expression on her face and said, 'Oh, Chelsea don't say *that*. You should ask how many are little boy kittens and how many are little girl kittens.'"

"What's the difference?" Connor asked.

"Well, exactly!" Chelsea rolled her eyes. "I mean, who cares, right? But no, it turns out that my grandmother has never in her life said the word 'sex' out loud, and she doesn't think I should either."

"What are you supposed to say?"

"I guess I'm supposed to spell it. Because

my grandmother said, 'Chelsea, I've never said S-E-X out loud in my life.'"

Connor started laughing.

"It's true!" Chelsea said, punching him in the arm. "It's a true story. Put that in your book."

"Sweetheart, for the zillionth time, it's a work of *fiction*. I refuse to keep going through it and having you point out inconsistencies." Connor started laughing again.

"What are you laughing about?" Chelsea asked.

"I was just thinking. . . . What does your grandmother think we do? Does she think I come up behind you in the kitchen and ask you if you want to come in the bedroom and have some S-E—"

The phone rang and Chelsea jumped up to answer it.

"Please stop talking about my grandmother and our sex life in the same sentence," she said over her shoulder. "It's entirely too disturbing and—Hello?" She interrupted herself to answer the phone.

"Justin?" she said. "How are—"

Her hand tightened on the phone.

"Tell me exactly what happened," she said, her voice staccato.

She listened, and then squeezed her eyes

closed for a minute. Connor got up quickly and crossed the room to reach her.

"Chelsea—" he whispered, but she only shook her head and gripped the telephone more tightly.

This is going to be really bad, Connor thought. *Whatever this is, it's the worst yet.*

Chelsea drove like a demon. It was a good thing for Connor that he got into the car and shut the door quickly, because she wouldn't have waited for him.

They got to the hospital in one piece (miraculously, in Connor's opinion). Chelsea parked the car so haphazardly that it took up three parking spaces, and then she marched into the hospital with such determination that Connor, whose legs were easily twice as long as hers, had to struggle to keep up.

Bang! Chelsea slapped open the first pair of glass doors. Connor followed her down the hall, watching her short skirt snap back and forth purposefully. How did Chelsea know where she was going? She didn't even pause at the admissions desk.

Bang! Chelsea whipped through another set of doors and rounded a corner.

Connor saw Grace holding hands with some skinny guy, Bo and Roan hugging each other, Marta, all looking pale and anxious. And there was Justin, dark hair still plastered to his skull, his face white as paper despite his tan, his eyes as haunted as a ghost's.

Chelsea saw none of them. Later she would be surprised to learn that they had gotten to the hospital before her. She thought only of Kate. She had thought only of Kate since Justin's phone call. She would never remember the drive to the hospital or be able to explain how she had found Kate's room. Later, she remembered nothing except throwing open the door to Kate's room and marching across the room to take her hand.

"It's okay now," Chelsea said to her unconscious friend in a voice that did not tremble. "It's going to be okay now."

Chelsea looks so grown up, Kate thought sleepily. *She looks like somebody's mom.*

Chelsea said something, but Kate couldn't hear it.

She looks so concerned, Kate thought. *Is that because Justin's dead?* She frowned.

Am I frowning? I can't feel it.

Chelsea said something else. Kate tried to hear. Finally she heard.

"Kate's in here," Chelsea said. *"She's dressed and she's in here by herself."*

"Justin's dead," Kate whispered. "He's dead and I'll never see him again."

She was in the dorm bathroom, wearing a robe and slippers. No one was around. She walked into the shower and turned it on—both spigots, full force. The water came at her hard, like a spray of needles. She turned her face upward, letting the water fill her mouth and run up her nose, letting it get in her eyes and swell the lids.

Someone shut the water off. Chelsea. Kate's soaked robe hung heavy on her shoulders. Chelsea's hands reached around from behind and turned her slowly.

"Justin's dead," Kate said, then reached again for the spigots. Chelsea caught her hands. Kate looked up at the shower head, longing to turn it on again, to drown the world around her. Why live in a world without Justin? She didn't want to cry, she wanted the shower to do it for her.

Chelsea held her hands. "Her eyes are open," she said. "Does that mean she can hear me?"

That doesn't make sense. Why would she say that?

"Justin's dead," Kate told Chelsea again.

"She looks like she—"

"—can hear," Chelsea was saying. "There's

105

a little line between her eyebrows, like she's concentrating."

"Well, you never know," said an unfamiliar, professional voice. "Most comatose patients awaken with no memory of anything that happened during the coma or even one or two days before the accident."

Comatose patients! Accident! Were they talking about her? No, surely not.

The strange, expert voice continued. "A few awaken with vague recollections of events that transpired while they were comatose." The voice paused. "And there have been cases where comatose patients recover and claim to have seen and heard everything." It was obvious that the owner of the voice did not believe this. Still, the voice said, "As a consequence, we encourage people to talk and act normally with comatose patients, because the truth is, we really don't know to what extent they are aware."

"I see," Chelsea said.

"Of course, you are under a lot of stress yourself, so if you find it difficult to talk to Kate naturally—"

Kate! So they were talking about her! Kate didn't feel much alarm. She was fascinated by this conversation in a very impersonal way.

"—you may find it easier to read a book to

her or sing a little song or tell riddles or whatever. Mainly, it is human contact that we encourage."

Please don't sing a little song, Chelsea, Kate thought.

"Thank you, Dr. Williams," Chelsea said, still speaking in her grave, serious voice.

That must be your hospital voice, Chels, Kate thought. *Nice and respectful.*

She heard footsteps retreating and other voices, but she drifted. Was that Grace she heard? Or Marta? She couldn't hear anymore. And was Justin dead or not? Why did she keep thinking that?

Suddenly she heard Chelsea again, speaking awkwardly in her hospital voice.

"Kate, it's me, Chelsea. . . . I thought I might read to you. . . . I went to the hospital library. . . . Okay, here we go." Chelsea cleared her throat. " 'Scarlett O'Hara was not beautiful but men seldom realized it when caught by her charm as the Tarleton twins were.' "

My God, she's reading Gone with the Wind, Kate thought. *That book is over a thousand pages long! How long does she expect me to be here?*

Unaware, Chelsea read on, her voice slowly gaining confidence and rhythm, the world diminishing to just the two of them.

107

EIGHT

Allegra reached the Seaside Motel with her paycheck—all $24.53 of it—burning a hole in her pocket. She lay on the lumpy mattress of room six and counted the cash in her hand. *Don't spend it all in one place*, she thought wryly. The woman at the day-care center had been appalled that Allegra had had the nerve to show up for her paycheck, but Allegra couldn't have cared less. She'd certainly earned it.

She still had some of the money Grace had lent her, plus this, and tomorrow she would have, hopefully, a quarter of a million dollars. So she supposed it wouldn't be splurging too terribly much to skip the egg salad sandwich at the diner and order a pizza.

She rolled over on her side and called Sam's Pizza from the bedside phone. "I'd like a small pizza with everything, and a large Coke," she said. "Delivered to the Seaside Motel, room six."

"The Seaside?" the guy at Sam's said. "Uh-uh. No way, lady. We don't deliver there."

"Why on earth not? You're just down the road."

"Too rough."

"What do you mean—too rough?"

"Too rough," the guy said. "Clientele, neighborhood, everything. I wouldn't want to send one of my people in there."

"Well, I'm here," Allegra said. "And *I'm* doing okay."

"You do sound like a nice person," the guy said, considering. "Okay, forty-five minutes." He hung up.

Allegra slammed down the phone. Honestly! She would be so happy to be rid of this whole town.

She took a quick shower, washing away the sand and salt of a day on the beach. She peered at her face anxiously in the mirror. Was all this sun exposure causing her to age prematurely?

There was a knock at the door. Allegra checked her watch. Only five minutes had

109

passed—Sam's certainly was prompt. She galloped to the door wearing a towel and shouting, "Hurray for Sam's brave boys!"

She threw open the door and caught her breath. A small man in a cream-colored suit stood in the doorway. Two men, each the approximate size of a refrigerator, stood on either side of him. Allegra knew that even if she slammed the door, one of those men could push the wall down just by leaning against it. There was no chance she could squeeze past them and run, either. And she certainly didn't think the Sam's Pizza delivery boy would be up for saving the day.

Allegra weighed her options. Her green eyes were cool and distant, her posture regal, despite the towel. She looked very much as though she hadn't a care in the world.

She could see this had some effect on the man in the cream-colored suit. He looked at her with grudging respect in his black eyes. His cream-colored fedora was in his hand with a flourish.

"Please excuse the interruption, Allegra," he said. He ran his eyes down the length of her body. "I seem to have caught you at a disadvantage."

Allegra shrugged her beautiful shoulders

with good grace. "Not at all," she said, stepping aside. "Won't you come in, Mr. Chernak?"

Half an hour later, as Chernak led her out to his car, his eyes were snapping blackly and Allegra's confidence was badly shaken. Chernak had found her quite by accident, he told her. "Beauties like you shouldn't go the beach," he said. "I was watching the beach from my hotel room and saw a flash of auburn hair and thought to myself, 'Why, that girl looks familiar. Why, that almost looks like *Allegra*—' "

"Oh, spare me," Allegra snapped, sick of his smug tone. "Watching girls through binoculars from your lonely hotel room is nothing to brag about."

The two refrigerator-sized men finished tossing her motel room.

"It's not here," one of them had said to Chernak.

"I didn't think it would be," Chernak had said thoughtfully. "But I wanted to be sure." He was sitting on the bed next to Allegra. He put his hand on her shoulder. "Get dressed, Chicken Little. We're going for a ride."

Allegra quickly pulled on shorts and a T-shirt, then said for the hundredth time,

"Chernak, if I had the drugs, would I be staying in a dump like this?"

Chernak led her out of the motel room to the car. He helped her into the backseat and slid in next to her. The two men got in front and maneuvered the big car out of the Seaside's parking lot.

"Say, boss, shouldn't you blindfold the little lady?" one of the men asked.

"Not to worry," Chernak said. "Allegra won't have much memory of this evening by the time we're through with her."

Chernak laid his arm companionably along the back of the car seat. "Now, Allegra, if you didn't have the drugs, I would think you'd be hustling your pretty little self down at the Ocean City Grande," he said, "trying to find some rich and lonely businessman. But since you seem relatively content to stay at—What was that place? The Seaside? Since you seem content to stay there, I suspect you know it's just of a matter of time. Have you found a buyer yet?"

"A buyer for what?"

Chernak sighed. "You are getting very tiresome," he said. "Or were you always very tiresome and I just failed to notice due to your not inconsiderable physical charms? I can't remember now."

112

"Chernak, I—"

"Shut up," he said easily. "You have some thinking to do. Be quiet until we get where we're going."

Allegra slid farther down against the car seat and did some thinking. By the time they got to the isolated beach house, she had a workable idea.

They walked from the car in silence. One of Chernak's men unlocked the door and ushered them inside. Chernak went into the kitchen and fixed himself a drink.

Allegra sat on the couch. Nobody seemed to really care what she did or where she went, which led her to believe that the cottage was very isolated indeed.

"Chernak?" she said.

"Yes, beautiful?" he called from the kitchen. His voice was too bright, too cheerful.

"I'm ready to tell you the truth," she called back.

"No one's stopping you."

"Okay . . ." Allegra paused. "You're right, I did smuggle some of the coke into the States—but not very much. Justin destroyed most of it."

"Aha!" Chernak said merrily. He brought his drink into the living room. "What a surprise, darling. Do continue."

113

Allegra locked her hands around her knees. "Well, you're not going to believe this, but someone stole the drugs from *me*."

"You're right. I don't believe you," Chernak said. He nodded to one of the men. "Bert, rip her head off."

Bert stood up, but Chernak laughed. "I'm joking," he said. "Tell me, darling, who stole the coke from you?"

Allegra swallowed, still looking at Bert. "Well, I don't know, or I would have gotten it back, but—"

"But?"

"Someone made a remark to me right after the coke was stolen. A guy on the beach said—said that he had something that belonged to me."

"A guy on the beach?" Chernak leaned forward.

"Yes, a—a skinny, sort of studious guy," Allegra said. "I've asked around about him. I think his name is William."

She saw the gleam in Chernak's eye. *So he isn't totally sure I have the coke*, she thought. *He knows who I'm talking about, and he really does think there's a chance that Wilton kept it.*

"William, William," Chernak said thoughtfully. "So that's why I haven't heard from him." He shook his head and looked back at her. "Well, thank you for being honest, Allegra. Bert will drive you home now."

"He will?" Allegra blurted out before she thought.

"Yes, my dear." Chernak looked at her shrewdly. "I don't want your untimely disappearance to alert this William that something's wrong. Don't leave town, though. You and I will have things to talk about when this is settled."

"That's it?" Allegra said. Relief rose through her like happiness, starting at her toes and soaring upward until it almost lifted her off her feet.

"Well, one more thing," Chernak said kindly. "Bert?"

Allegra turned, and Bert drove his encyclopedia-sized fist into her sternum, driving air and consciousness from her in one expert move.

Grace flicked on the kitchen light and sighed. The others crowded into the house behind her. Roan was sniffling.

"Roan, please don't cry," Grace said. "If you cry, I'll cry, and who knows where that may end."

Roan gave her a small, watery little smile.

"That's better," Grace said. "Now, why don't you both get some sleep?"

"We have to walk Mooch first," Bo said.

"Oh, jeez, that's right, I'd forgotten all about poor Mooch," Grace said. "Where is he?"

"Probably sleeping on Justin and Kate's bed," Roan said. She went to the bottom of the stairs and whistled. They heard the muted jingling of Mooch's collar tags, and then Mooch himself thumped down the stairs.

Roan snapped the leash on Mooch, and she and Bo went out the back door.

Grace stretched. "Want to sit on the porch?" she asked Wilton.

"Sure." He nodded. "But let me make you something to eat first."

"I'm not hungry."

"I know, but you need to eat."

Grace put a hand to her head. "Wilton, please, please don't get all motherly on me right now."

"Sorry, but you do need to eat." Wilton opened the refrigerator and peered around. "However, you're in luck, because I don't think you should eat anything out of this refrigerator. How often do you guys clean this thing out?"

Grace smiled despite herself. "Every once in a while."

"Yeah, well, I think it might be time right now," Wilton said, poking around experimentally. "There are vegetables playing three-card monte in the back." He shut the refrigerator door. "Come on, I'll buy you dinner at the Hamilton Diner."

Grace threw up her hands. "Wilton, I don't want dinner. I want to sit on the porch and have some peace and quiet. With you. Okay? Please?"

Wilton looked at her for a minute. "Okay," he said.

They went out on the porch and settled comfortably on the porch swing. Grace rested her head against Wilton's shoulder.

"Better?" Wilton asked.

"Mmm." Grace's eyes were closed. "Much better."

Wilton tucked a lock of Grace's hair behind her ear. "Kate must be a very close friend," he said softly.

Grace half-smiled. "I don't know if you could say that," she said. "It might be more accurate to say that we've been through a lot together."

Wilton continued to stroke her hair. "Jeez, that guy at the hospital," he said. "He looks like he's been soaking his eyeballs in lemon juice or something."

Grace winced when she thought of Justin's eyes, so bloodshot, so scared. "Justin?" she asked. "Well, he loves Kate more than anything in the world. She's the most important thing in his life." She sighed. "Imagine losing someone that close to you."

"Hey, you haven't lost her yet," Wilton said. "I don't think Kate would like everyone to be planning what to wear to her funeral."

"You don't even know her," Grace protested.

"True, but if I were in a coma, I certainly wouldn't want all my friends hanging crepe already," Wilton said.

There was a flash of lightning on the horizon. Grace suddenly noticed that the air was heavy and humid. It was going to storm.

He stood up. "Grace, you're going to bed." He held out his hand.

"Is this a seduction?" Grace smiled as she took his hand and stood up.

Wilton rolled his eyes. "No, it's not a seduction," he said. "But it's late and you're exhausted and need to rest. So go inside and go to bed."

"Okay," Grace said, yawning.

Wilton hugged her. "Listen, to continue a conversation that we were having about ten hours ago? I know I've been preoccupied

118

lately, but it's nothing for you to worry about."

Lightning flashed again. He kissed her gently on the lips. "It's because I've fallen in love with you," Wilton said softly.

Then, before Grace could reply, he leaped off the porch, nearly catching his foot on the railing and yelping in surprise as he landed in a rosebush. He yanked himself free and raced across the lawn, a tall, embarrassed figure illuminated by the lightning.

Justin leaned against the wall next to the pay phone. He was drinking lukewarm coffee from a Styrofoam cup.

He watched a nurse walk by, then a doctor, then another nurse. *Okay*, he told himself, *when three doctors have walked by, I'll call.*

Two minutes later, three doctors had walked by. Justin started to revise his game. *When three doctors with stethoscopes around their necks—*

He shook his head. He had to call. No more stalling. He took the last swig of coffee, then picked up the phone and dialed the operator for information in Kate's hometown.

"Residence or business?" the operator asked.

"Residence."

119

"Yes?"

"Um, I need the number for . . ." Justin paused. What was Kate's father's name? He blanked. "For Mr. Quinn," he said at last.

"First name?"

"I can't remember."

"Do you have the address, sir?"

"No, I'm sorry."

The operator gave a long, annoyed sigh. "I have eighteen Quinns listed. I'm going to need a first name or an address."

"Look, I can't remember, but it's urgent that I get the number. Can you read me the first names?" Justin said. "I'll know the right one when I hear it."

Another sigh from the operator. "Quinn, Arthur," she began. "Quinn, Christopher. Quinn, Gerald. Quinn, MacDonald. Quinn, Michael. Quinn, Paul. . . ."

As it turned out, Justin *didn't* know the name when he heard it. He picked the four names that sounded reasonably familiar: Gerald, MacDonald, Stuart, and Walter. He pulled a pen out of his back pocket and scratched the numbers on the side of the Styrofoam cup. Then he thanked the operator and hung up. Chelsea and Connor had given him a stack of coins, and he took them out of the pocket of his windbreaker.

Gerald Quinn was not at home.

Stuart Quinn sounded nineteen years old, and when Justin asked him if he had a daughter named Kate, Stuart's voice became very guarded, and he said, "No, is someone claiming I fathered a daughter?"

Walter Quinn said, "Son, I lost my wife in 'forty-five and we were never blessed with children," in such an accusing tone that Justin felt obliged to tell the man that he was sorry for his loss.

A woman answered the phone at MacDonald Quinn's home. "Hello?"

"Hello," Justin said. "Could I speak to MacDonald, please?"

"Certainly. May I tell him who's calling?"

Justin hesitated. "Is this Mrs. Quinn?"

"Yes. Who is this?"

"Mrs. Quinn, this is Justin Garrett." He paused, waiting for her to recognize his name.

"Justin, how are you? What's going on? Is something wrong?" She swallowed, and even over the phone Justin heard the nervous *click* in her throat. He had frightened her. He was really handling this beautifully. "Has something happened to Kate?"

Again, Justin hesitated. "Maybe I should speak to Mr. Quinn," he said.

121

"Whatever it is, you can tell me," Kate's mother said. "I'm not a hysterical person."

Taking her at her word, Justin began talking.

Roan shivered as she trotted along the beach after Mooch, Bo beside her.

"Cold?" Bo asked, putting his arm around her.

"Yes," Roan said. "I mean, no."

Bo laughed. "Which is it?"

"I don't know!" Roan said so plaintively that the smile faded from Bo's face. "I don't know why I'm shivering, unless it's because I'm so scared."

"Scared for Kate?"

Roan nodded.

"She'll be okay, Roan."

"You don't know that! She might not be okay at all! She might—"

"Shhh," Bo said. "Don't say it."

"Why not?" Roan said. "I'm thinking it. We're all thinking it. Did you get a look at Justin's face?"

Bo sighed. He pulled Roan closer and slowed their pace. Mooch was practically yanking her arm out of the socket, but Bo took no notice. "Roan," he said softly. "We have to believe that Kate's going to be okay,

122

because I can't bear to think about losing another person I love. Okay?"

Roan nodded.

Bo kissed her very gently. "And no matter what happens, you have me," he said. "And I have you."

Roan smiled faintly. "Oh, definitely," she whispered. "You definitely have me. Now let's keep walking before Mooch chokes himself on the end of the leash."

Bo took Roan's free hand. "The wind is picking up," he said.

She nodded. The wind *was* picking up. It blew needlelike sprays of sand into their faces, and soon Roan *was* shivering from the cold, but Mooch bounded along, happy and oblivious.

Lucky Mooch, thought Roan.

Allegra awoke slowly, aware of nothing but the huge raw pain that was her chest. Out of instinct, she panted, knowing that taking a deeper breath might cause her to pass out again.

She was lying on her side in darkness. After a long time, she rolled—slowly, slowly—onto her back. Her injured ribs and lungs expanded slightly and she felt a little better. She realized she that she was in her room at the Seaside.

So Chernak let me come home after all, she thought. *But he gave me a warning not to leave town, didn't he?*

She raised herself up off the bed carefully, trying to keep her chest horizontal as long as possible. She looked like she was trying to balance an egg on her stomach. She went into the bathroom and lifted her T-shirt, wincing. A magnificent black bruise was flowering on her chest, the outer edges of it green and yellow.

Oh, great. How am I supposed to pull off a drug deal on the beach tomorrow? she thought. *Well, I guess I could wear a scarf or something. . . . A scarf with a bathing suit? Who am I kidding? I'll have to wear a T-shirt over my suit.*

Allegra took a deeper breath and was surprised and relieved to find that it didn't hurt that much. No broken ribs. That was lucky. Maybe Bert was trained to hit people that way—hard enough to bruise but not hard enough to break bones.

The phone rang while Allegra was stretching experimentally. Lifting her arms was painful, but otherwise she seemed okay.

The phone rang again. *That'll be Chernak or Sam's Pizza*, she thought. She crossed the room and picked up the receiver.

"Is this Allegra Wolfe? This is Luis Salgado."

"Hello, Mr. Salgado." Allegra sighed. Luis, the head lifeguard, the Man the Shark Forgot. What was he bothering her for?

"I'm sorry to call so late," Luis said. "But Justin Garrett and Kate Quinn gave me your name about a week ago as someone who might be interested in lifeguarding."

"I'm sorry, but I already have a job," Allegra lied. *And anyway, I sure wouldn't want to risk my neck saving a bunch of tourists*, she thought.

"I see," Luis said. "I was just hoping you could help me out. There was an accident today and—"

"Oh, I'm not trained to lifeguard, anyway. Hey, what happened at the beach? No one seemed to know," Allegra said. *I was setting up the particulars of a drug deal and missed all the excitement*, she added to herself.

"There was a Jet Ski accident," Luis said. "Kate Quinn received a serious head trauma."

"I'm sorry to hear that," Allegra said automatically. "Does she have a concussion? Maybe I'll give her a call. Is she at home?"

"No," Luis said shortly. "She's in I.C.U. at the hospital in a coma from which she may or may not emerge."

And he hung up.

● ● ●

Wilton raced across Grace's lawn. He'd said he loved her! He'd said he loved her!

You idiot, he thought. What was he doing, telling a girl like Grace he was in love with her? She probably heard that two or three times a week.

He jogged down the driveway, arms akimbo. He had a fleeting glimpse of something, a shadow out of place in the yard. Was someone there? He shook his head. He was paranoid, thinking that people were lurking around, waiting to hear the Love Confessions of a Teenage Werewolf.

Wilton ran faster, trying to outrun his embarrassment. He had completely forgotten that he'd left his car at Grace's house.

Suddenly Wilton thought again of the shadow on Grace's lawn, and a chill ran down his spine. Could Chernak be following him? Wilton had been waiting for Chernak to contact him. He planned to tell Chernak that he couldn't find any drugs in Allegra's room. But maybe Chernak already knew? Maybe—

Wilton put on a final burst of speed and flew through the door of his parents' condo. His mother was standing at the kitchen counter, and she winced as the door slammed behind him.

"Good heavens, Wilton," she said. "You act like the hounds of hell are after you. I don't know what's come over you lately."

Allegra stomped around her room for a while, thinking of Luis saying, *Kate's in I.C.U. at the hospital in a coma from which she may or may not emerge.*

Yeah, well, *all* people in comas may or may not emerge, she thought. So what was she supposed to do? Show up at the hospital with a tin of cookies? She was the last person Kate or Justin—who was no doubt sitting patiently at Kate's side—would want to see. Still . . . Allegra looked at the phone thoughtfully. She picked it up and dialed.

"Hello?"

"Grace? It's me . . . Allegra."

"Oh, hi," Grace said. Her voice sounded small and hollow.

"Grace, I heard about Kate, and—" Allegra paused. She wished she knew what to say. So she said, "I wish I knew what to say."

"I know what you mean," Grace said. She sighed. "Everyone's gone to bed and the house is so quiet. . . . Now there's nothing to do but think about—Kate."

Allegra hesitated. "Is there—is there anything I can do?"

"I don't think there's anything any of us can do," Grace said.

"No, I meant is there anything I can do for *you*," Allegra said.

There was a very slight pause. "No, I'll be okay," Grace said. "But I'm glad you called."

And she, like Luis, hung up, but Allegra didn't mind.

Grace hung up the phone and wandered through the house, turning off lights. So maybe Allegra did have some human decency after all. Kate would be surprised to hear that. Grace frowned. That is, Kate would be surprised if she lived to hear it.

She went upstairs to her room. She dropped her clothes on the floor, pulled on a nightgown, and slid into bed. She just wanted to sleep. Maybe tomorrow she would wake up and find that none of this had happened. Well, except for the part of Wilton saying he loved her. That could still have happened. She smiled and snuggled deeper into her bed. In no time at all she was sound asleep.

She woke up fifteen minutes later when a heavy hand clamped down over her mouth and a thick voice said, "Don't move a muscle."

NINE

The man kept his hand over Grace's mouth while another man used duct tape to bind her feet together. Another piece across her mouth, then they flipped her over and taped her hands together behind her back.

Grace didn't struggle. These men were the size of small cars; fighting them wouldn't do a bit of good.

"All right," one of them whispered. "Upsy-daisy." And he lifted her with one arm, exerting no more effort than a person picking up a book.

My God, part of Grace's brain thought. *This guy is incredibly strong. Did he really just say "upsy-daisy"?*

Quickly, quietly, they carried Grace through the house. How could such big men move so silently? Why didn't someone else in the house wake up and start screaming? Or call the police?

Outside, the wind had picked up and the hem of Grace's baby-doll nightgown fluttered briskly as they crossed the street. The man holding her dumped her unceremoniously into the backseat of a car, and both men got into the front seat.

Grace twisted around until she was on her back. She tried to memorize the turns they were taking so that she could figure out their location, but it was impossible. Lightning flashed, and in the glare Grace saw that one of the men was looking at her. She tried to imprint his face on her memory from just that split-second view.

Then suddenly she wanted to scream. The men hadn't blindfolded her, which meant that they were sure she wasn't going to live long enough to ever pick them out of a lineup.

Kate drifted. She wanted to be in the real world, but couldn't quite get there. There seemed to be some sort of veil in the way, some membrane she couldn't get through. Earlier, she had listened to Chelsea read from *Gone with the Wind*, and she had felt so *close*.

She couldn't believe that Chelsea didn't realize how close to consciousness she was. But Chelsea read on, oblivious, and now Kate was tired of trying.

And where was Justin? She hadn't heard him, hadn't seen him. And now she was so tired . . . but she wanted to see him so much.

Kate peered through the billowing steam in the bathroom. She edged the door farther open. Another cloud of steam escaped, swirling around a guy barely covered by the towel wrapped around his waist. Water dripped off his dark hair onto the floor. She could tell by the rough stubble of beard that he hadn't gotten around to shaving this morning.

He glanced at her sourly, but suddenly the annoyance in his eyes vanished. His face went completely blank. He continued to stare.

"Justin?" Kate said.

His eyes were still locked on hers. She wasn't sure what she saw in them. Shock? Hurt? Anger?

"I can't believe it's you," she said, to fill the silence and to silence the sob in her throat.

"Believe it," he said. He took a step closer, so close that drops from his hair spilled onto her shirt, so close she could smell the fresh scent of his soap, she could see the uncertainty in his eyes.

So close that when he reached for her and pulled her against his wet, hard chest and kissed her, it seemed like the only thing in the world that he could have done.

It was the kiss she'd remembered, the one that made her forget who she was. But there was something different in the way Justin touched her, an urgency that she hadn't remembered. His hands on her shoulders were gripping too tightly, his kiss was too searching. It wasn't right. It wasn't the same. She started to pull away and he let her go instantly.

For a moment they stared at each other. Then Justin shook his head, backed into the bathroom, and closed the door.

Kate was crying. At least she thought she was crying, she wanted to be crying, but it was hard to tell when she couldn't feel the tears on her face.

The man carried Grace into the abandoned beach house as easily as he'd carried her out of her own house. He and the other man took her into a small room and tied her to a hardback chair. When double loops of thick rope were wrapped across her chest, waist, and legs, they ripped off the piece of duct tape that covered her mouth.

"Ouch," Grace said mildly.

"Sorry," one of them said automatically. Then he suddenly seemed self-conscious about apologizing and glanced quickly at the other man to see if he had noticed.

The other man didn't seem interested. "Look, you know what to do, right?" he said. "I'll be back in a little while," and he left the room.

The man who'd apologized called, "Okay, Bert," and began bustling around, in and out of the room, getting organized. He got a bottle of bourbon out and took a drink, then began reading the directions to a Polaroid camera.

His head looked too small for his body, but then maybe he had such a huge body that any head would look too small. He actually looked a great deal like Grace's old piano teacher, Mr. Harriman.

"Okay," not-quite-Mr. Harriman said, putting down the directions and picking up the camera. He pointed it at Grace. "Say cheese."

"What are you talking about?"

"Okay, don't say cheese. Say 'What are you talking about?'" Mr. Harriman snapped the camera. "There we go," he said conversationally. He sat down at a table and watched the picture develop, drinking from the bourbon bottle.

"This should do," he said at last. "We just

need some evidence so that your boyfriend will believe we're holding you."

"Boyfriend?" Grace said, startled.

Mr. Harriman laughed. "What—do you have more than one? I'll bet you do."

Grace thought furiously. Did he mean Wilton? But what did Wilton have to do with *this*? She couldn't exactly imagine him having lots of underworld contacts.

Still, they were holding her hostage, but they didn't seem ready to kill her—yet—or to use her in some weird film. And Mr. Harriman didn't seem *that* menacing if you could get past the size of him.

Mr. Harriman caught her looking at the bottle of bourbon. "You like bourbon?" he asked. "Well, maybe we can work something out later."

"I don't want any bourbon," Grace said, but her voice cracked a little bit.

"Well, you may change your mind," Mr. Harriman said. "And if you do . . . well, you be nice to me, I'll be nice to you."

Grace saw that his gaze was resting on her shoulder. The strap of her nightgown had slipped. She shuddered. Maybe Mr. Harriman was more than menacing enough after all. The real Mr. Harriman had never looked at her like that.

• • •

Justin met Kate's parents at the admissions desk. He shook hands with them. MacDonald Quinn had a square, determined jaw, which he had passed on to his daughter.

Kate's mother had beautiful blue eyes. Tonight they were shadowed by fear. "Has there been any change?" she asked anxiously.

Justin shook his head. "I'm sorry. She's still in a coma."

They began walking down the hall. "Tell us again what happened," Kate's father said.

Justin tried to clear his head. He was thinking about the time he'd stepped out of the bathroom to find that Kate had moved into the big house. He remembered kissing her. Why couldn't he stop thinking about that?

Kate's father was staring at him.

Justin made an effort to be clear and coherent. "Two Jet Skiers collided," he said. "Kate and I swam out—"

"You swam out when there were motorized vehicles in the water?" Kate's father snapped.

"Yes. We—" Justin faltered. "The patrol boat was too far away—we—we had to get there—"

"What do you mean, you had to?" Kate's

father said. "You had to expose yourselves to danger like that? You—"

"It's their job, Mr. Quinn," a soft voice said from behind them. Justin turned to see Marta in her wheelchair. Her face was worried but determined. "Kate and Justin went into the water because that was the best alternative," she said firmly.

Mr. Quinn looked at Marta sternly; then his face relaxed. "You must be Marta," he said, and shook her hand.

Marta shook hands with Kate's mother, also, and began wheeling down the hall next to them. "I know how you feel," she said softly. "An accident like Kate's or mine can cause so many recriminations, but right now you have to focus on Kate and what she's going through."

Mr. Quinn put his arm around Mrs. Quinn. Marta glanced at Justin over her shoulder, and he gave her a grateful look. But he fell behind as they headed for Kate's room.

He wondered if he and Kate *had* chosen the best alternative. Maybe they should have waited for the patrol boat. But it had been so far away. What was Luis going to say? Maybe if Justin had seen the other boy before Kate did . . . He shook his head.

He walked along the corridor, taking his time. He thought about Kate's dead sister,

Julianna. He was not anxious to catch up to Kate's parents and hear them try to comfort their remaining child.

The doorbell to Wilton's parents' condo rang at midnight, and Wilton jumped and spilled a bowl of popcorn.

"Oh, for heaven's sake," his mother said. "You are so jumpy these days."

"Sorry," Wilton said.

"Well, it's nothing to be sorry about," his mother said, sweeping up popcorn. "I'm just worried about you, is all."

Wilton's father looked at them over the top of his newspaper. "Yes, you have been a little out of sorts, Wilton," he said. "Yesterday at breakfast your hands were shaking so badly I thought you were going to spill the orange juice."

"Are you in love?" his mother asked dreamily. Her eyes misted behind her glasses.

"Mom—"

"In love?" Wilton's father put the paper aside in favor of this conversation. "Who's he in love with?"

"Her name is Grace," his mother continued rapturously. "And she's *beautiful*."

"Hey, how do you know about her?" Wilton asked.

"I saw you two talking on the beach today," his mother said. "I was bringing you a sack lunch."

Wilton closed his eyes, briefly thanking God that his mother hadn't sashayed up with a paper bag while he was talking to Grace. "Look—" he started.

"So I asked someone who she was and I wrote her a letter this afternoon," his mother said.

"You *what*?"

"I wrote her a letter, asking her to Sunday dinner," his mother said. Her eyes had a faraway look. "I said that we were very interested in meeting Wilton's friends—"

"I'm going to kill myself," Wilton said aloud. He was privately planning a midnight robbery of the post office.

"I must say, this is all just fascinating," Wilton's father said.

The doorbell rang again.

His mother frowned. "I was hoping they'd go away," she said. "Go answer it, will you, sweetie?" she said to Wilton. "It might be"— she paused dramatically—"Grace."

"Oh, for heaven's sake," Wilton said. He stomped down the hall and threw open the door. His jaw dropped.

A huge man filled the doorway. Lightning

138

flashed behind him, silhouetting him. It was the scariest sight Wilton had ever seen.

The man smiled almost genially. "Hello, Wilton," he said.

"Hello," Wilton said warily.

The big man put a hand against the door jamb, as though casually planning to push the house down. "Mr. Chernak has a message for you," he said. "He says he wants the drugs."

"I don't have the—"

The man pressed something into Wilton's hand. "Find them," he said simply, and walked off into the night.

Wilton stared at the object the man had given him.

"Wilton," his mother called. "Who's there?"

Wilton didn't answer. He was still staring at the object. It was a Polaroid snapshot of Grace.

Kate felt like she was tossing and turning, but part of her knew that she wasn't moving at all. Still, she was so restless. Where was Justin? She wanted more than anything to see Justin.

Lightning flashed outside her room. Some part of Kate's brain registered it. Storming? Was it—

A jagged bolt of lightning turned the world brilliant as the sun. In an explosion of thunder, a nearby tree flew apart, the sparks quickly extinguished by the rain.

She screamed in terror. "I'm going to die," she said aloud, willing herself to accept it. There was no escape. She had no control any longer. All she could do was wait for the next bolt of lightning to find her.

Headlights swept across her, more steady than the flashing lightning, and suddenly Justin was there, drenched, squinting in the rain, but there. They fought the wind all the way back to the Jeep. Then they were inside, the rain pelting the thin roof. Justin turned the heater on.

"You found me," Kate said at last, breathing slowly, tentatively, as if she had forgotten how.

"You're alive," Justin said,

Kate nodded. "I almost gave up."

"But you didn't." Justin smiled and brushed away a tear. "You know we can't get out of here tonight. We'll have to ride it out here in the Jeep."

In the morning, Kate was sore and hungry and ached in every joint, but she was absolutely alone, as if she were plugged into some inexhaustible power source.

"How can I ever thank you for saving my

life?" she asked Justin playfully. "For rescuing me from a hurricane?"

"Well, I . . ."

"Don't argue, all right?" Kate said, stepping closer.

"You've had a bad night," Justin said gently. "Maybe you should think this over."

"You think I'm just stressed out?" Kate asked, softly mocking. She touched his side. The hard muscles there quivered in response. "That's not it, Justin."

He gave up resisting and raised his hand to her cheek, his touch as gentle and warm as the breeze. "I just thought I'd give you a chance to change your mind," he said.

"I don't want a chance." Kate lifted her T-shirt with both hands.

Justin moved closer, slowly pressing his chest against her. Thighs skimmed, hips brushed, fingers laced. His skin was so smooth, so hot . . .

Lightning flashed again. Kate tried to remember where she was, why she couldn't open her eyes. She was so tired. Was it from the night in the hurricane? The lightning again. Maybe she was still in the hurricane. *Justin*, she thought. *Please come rescue me again.*

• • •

In the corner of Kate's room, asleep in a hard green plastic chair, Justin jumped awake when the thunder crashed.

Jesus. He ran a hand through his salt-stiff hair. He needed to shave, and his eyes felt like they were being rubbed with sandpaper.

More thunder and then lightning. Justin frowned. He'd been dreaming. Something about Hurricane Barbara and the time he'd found Kate. . . . He wrinkled his brow, but the dream slipped away.

He stretched and went out into the hall for some air, but the air in the hall was just as still and thick as it was in Kate's room. He walked down the corridor to the double set of glass doors that led to the parking lot. It was raining so heavily that it looked like an opaque gray wall began a few feet outside the door. He leaned his forehead against the cool glass.

He thought once more about Hurricane Barbara. It had been happening all day— memories would insert themselves in his consciousness, and he was helpless to shake them. He figured it must be the stress.

"Justin?"

He turned to see Marta. He smiled faintly. "Marta, what are you still doing here?"

"Oh, I had some work to catch up on at

142

the clinic," she said. "Besides, I'd rather stay late and sleep in the on-call room than go out in this storm."

Justin sighed. "I don't know how you can take this place," he said.

"Oh, you get used to it," she said lightly, and Justin realized that Marta must've spent weeks in a hospital bed after she'd been shot. And now she worked in one.

"I'm sorry, Marta," he said. "That was stupid of me. . . . Listen, I wanted to thank you for what you said to Kate's parents earlier."

"What I said applies to you, too," Marta said. "This is no time for recriminations, Justin."

"I know, but—it's just so senseless!" Justin said. "Everything was going so smoothly, and now Kate's in a coma? How did that happen? How *could* that happen?"

Marta wheeled her chair closer and took his hand. "That's exactly what I'm talking about," she said. "You can't think about what could have been. You have to help Kate now."

"There's nothing I *can* do for her now, Marta," Justin said. "I should have done something this afternoon, when—"

"Jeez, I'm talking to a brick wall," Marta said mildly. "Didn't I just tell you not to dwell on the past?"

"Yes, but—"

"So why don't you go to Kate's room and hold her hand and tell her that you love her and you always will, no matter what?"

"Because—" Justin started, and then stopped. He leaned down and kissed Marta's forehead. "You are the smartest person I have ever met."

Marta smiled. "Thanks, but I don't recall a lot of competition. Who am I up against? Mooch?"

Justin kissed her again and walked back down the hall to Kate's room. He stood by the bed, holding her hand.

"I love you, kiddo," he said quietly. There was no change, absolutely no change.

He curled up again in his chair, and sat staring, dry-eyed, at the wall.

Allegra answered the door with sleep blearing her pretty green eyes, her hand rubbing absently at her chest. She squinted. "Wilton?"

Wilton dashed past her into the room. He wore a raincoat that was about three sizes too big for him. His hair was plastered to his skull by the rain, and his eyes were so wild they were practically rolling.

"What is it?" Allegra asked, more alertly.

"Chernak," Wilton gasped. He swallowed. "Chernak's got Grace and he's going to kill her if we don't give him the coke." He shrugged out of the raincoat. Allegra saw that he wore pajamas underneath. They were pale blue with a pattern of little horses embroidered in dark blue. He tried to wipe the water from his glasses with his fingers.

"Again, please," Allegra said. She gave his pajamas another look up and down, then sat on the bed and crossed her legs.

Wilton took a deep breath. "Chernak has Grace—and he's going to kill her—unless we give him the drugs."

Allegra raised an eyebrow. "We?"

"Damn it, Allegra! This is no time for games. He's going to kill Grace!" Wilton's voice cracked.

"Don't fly off the handle, Wilton," Allegra said calmly. "It doesn't become you."

"Allegra—"

"I sympathize with you, Wilton, I really do," Allegra said. "But I can't give you the coke."

"You *what*?"

"I've already sold it."

"You already—You can't have—" Wilton's face was white as sugar. Suddenly he narrowed his eyes. "You're lying."

"I am not," Allegra protested. "Look, I'm very fond of Grace, too. I certainly would give you the drugs if I still had them, but I don't."

Wilton smiled grimly. "So then give me the money."

"What are you talking about?"

"Give me the money," Wilton repeated. "Chernak doesn't care whether it's cocaine or cash, so give me the money and we'll work it out."

"I don't have the cash," Allegra said. She made her face carefully blank. "It's being deposited into a numbered account in the Bahamas. I can't get to it until I go there in person and—"

Wilton was next to her before she knew it. He poked a finger at her chest. Allegra winced.

"You're lying," he said hoarsely. "You're going to let Grace *die*."

"Wilton—"

He was pulling the raincoat on over his horsie pajamas. Allegra thought she had never seen anything quite so heartbreaking in all her life.

"Wilton, all I can tell you is to go to Chernak and plead your case," she said.

"Thanks for your compassion," Wilton said harshly.

146

"Wilton—"

But he was gone, slamming the door so hard that it came halfway off its rusty hinges, and the rain gusted in to soak Allegra where she stood.

TEN

The membrane between Kate and the rest of the world was getting thicker. She rarely broke though it now.

Once, she thought she heard somebody saying, "Sir, can I get you anything? Coffee? No? Well, why don't you rest then? Sir? Sir. . . . No, I guess you can stay here." Kate wondered who was talking. Must be a nurse. And who were they talking to? "Sir"? Who was that?

She floated gently. Things grew darker and lighter, then darker again. She didn't hear things in the real world anymore.

The morning dawned crystal clear and bright. Kate could hear a breeze blowing past her window, a fresh wind blowing out of the south. Perfect weather for sailing, A perfect, perfect day for Justin to sail away.

It was still early, but she knew he would be

leaving with the tide, heading northeast to Nantucket, then away across the sea.

She dressed in shorts and a bathing-suit top. What do you wear to say good-bye to your first love? How did she want him to remember her? Did she want him to remember her at all?

By the time she walked down to the boathouse, he'd already brought the boat out and tied it to the dock, bow facing the house. Mooch, sensing the excitement, was running around like a crazed puppy. Grace was handing Justin last-minute supplies from the dock—fresh fruit and vegetables, and real milk that would later be replaced by powdered.

They were busy, the two of them, and Justin went below as Kate stepped onto the dock. She opened the boathouse door and went inside. It was the same drafty, damp barn, and yet totally changed. Somehow Justin's presence was already fading away. She climbed the stairs to the loft and sat on the bare mattress.

It seemed like forever that she sat there, remembering. When he appeared at her side, she was surprised. She hadn't heard him call her name.

Justin sat down beside her and for a while he shared her silence. Somehow his hand found hers, and the tears fell freely.

"I feel like hell," he said at last.

"Yeah."

"Was there ever any way it could have worked?" he asked.

Kate smiled bitterly. There was a painful lump at the back of her throat. "I think we both knew all along," she said in a low voice. "Maybe that's why it was so . . . so wonderful."

"It was wonderful." He threaded his strong fingers through hers. "Are you sorry? Do you wish we'd never happened?"

Kate bit her lip and shook her head. "No, Justin. I'll never, never be sorry."

"Wherever I go, wherever I am—" he began, before his voice broke.

"I know," Kate whispered.

Chelsea and Connor were waiting out on the dock, holding hands and looking sleepy. Grace was wrapped in David's arms, exchanging her own whispered good-byes.

Justin kept his eyes low and climbed aboard his boat.

At last, with many final touches, many sad looks, Grace pulled away from David. She started to climb into the boat, then stopped herself. She came over to Kate, a sad, wry smile on her lips.

"You okay?" Grace asked.

"I'll live."

"Of course you will. You're the Golden Girl."

"Yeah, that's me," Kate said.

"Kind of, uh, you know—make sure David's all right, will you?" Grace asked. "You guys could have him over for one of Chelsea's awful spaghetti dinners or something."

"No problem," Kate said. "And you, too. You know. Maybe you could write me sometime. No, no, don't."

"I will," Grace assured her. She hesitated for a moment. "I'll miss you, Kate."

"Will you?" Kate asked, smiling. "Why? We're not the best of friends, are we?"

"Absolutely not," Grace said. "But we've been the very best of enemies."

She turned and hopped aboard the boat. Mooch ran to the bow and barked. Justin cast off the lines and revved the engine till the boat began to sidle slowly from the dock.

He raised his hand and waved. Kate waved back.

The sun reflecting off the water hurt her eyes.

Good-bye. Good-bye . . . *Justin?* Kate thought. She was all alone in her dark cocoon. *Good-bye, Justin, wherever you are.* She drifted farther away.

"I don't know any jokes," Mr. Harriman was saying. "You tell another one."

"Surely you must know some jokes,"

Grace said. Her voice was sweet, teasing, but she felt like screaming. They had been doing this for hours. "Everyone knows jokes."

Mr. Harriman scowled. "Not me," he said. He took another drink out of the bourbon bottle. "You tell one," he said sullenly.

"Okay," Grace said smoothly, quickly. "How is a man like kitchen linoleum?" Then she remembered the punch line to that joke and realized she didn't want to tell it to Mr. Harriman.

Mr. Harriman smiled tipsily. "I don't know," he said. "How?"

"Untie my hands and I'll tell you," Grace said.

To her surprise, Mr. Harriman threw back his head and laughed. "Okay, dearest," he said with mock courtesy.

He walked behind her and undid her hands. Grace rubbed her arms. They were numb.

Mr. Harriman walked back to his chair and sat down heavily. "You know why I did that?" he said to Grace.

"To hear the punch line to my joke."

"Wrong!" Mr. Harriman said heartily. "I untied your hands because it doesn't matter if your hands are untied."

"I—"

"Because supposing you untied your *feet*, then supposing you untie your *legs*." Mr. Harriman said *laigs*. "Then supposing you get past *me*, then supposing you get past *Bert* in the next room, where will you go?"

"I'm not trying—"

"Because there's no place *to* go," Mr. Harriman said. For a very brief moment he looked perfectly sober. "We're twenty miles from the nearest neighbor," he said without slurring. Then he hiccuped.

"Besides," he said. "I thought you might want a drink." He held out the bottle.

"I don't want a drink," Grace said. *Oh, but I do*, she thought. *I want a drink so much that I would gladly drink out of the bottle that Mr. Harriman has put his greasy lips on.*

"Come on," Mr. Harriman said. "I know you want a drink. I can see it in your eyes."

That's true, Grace thought. *I'm sure that's completely true.*

"I don't want a drink," she said again. "I don't drink, I don't like to drink."

"Well, maybe you should reconsider it," Mr. Harriman said leaning back in his chair. "We could have a few drinks, get to know each other better." His eyes traveled the length of her body in the baby-doll nightgown.

Why did I ever buy this thing, anyway? Grace thought. *If I get out of here, I will sleep in flannel granny nightgowns the rest of my life. With a gun under my pillow.*

"I said—"

"I heard what you said," Mr. Harriman said. "And you heard what I said. So think about it. Because you're not going to get yourself out of here by sweet-talking me with jokes all night."

Grace smiled wryly. *He's a lot smarter than you think he is*, she told herself, *so watch it.*

Mr. Harriman was still staring at her *laigs* in a thoughtful way. He started to say something, but Bert called to him from the other room.

"Just a minute," he called back. He pressed the bourbon bottle into one of Grace's hands, wrapping her fingers around it drunkenly. "There you go," he said. "You just take a drink while I'm gone and we'll see what we can work out when I get back."

He patted her on the shoulder with one of his meaty hands and left the room, lurching slightly.

Grace looked at the bourbon bottle in her hands. She wasn't sure that if she drank all the booze in the world, she would get drunk enough to "work something out" with Mr.

Harriman. But then again, how strong was her desire to die here?

If Mr. Harriman wanted her drunk, perhaps that's what she should do. And wouldn't being drunk make whatever was coming much easier for her? She just didn't know.

Holding the bourbon bottle tighter, she lowered her head and began to cry.

Allegra didn't think she'd get back to sleep, what with her door hanging half off the hinges, wind swirling around the room, and the prospect of another visit from Chernak or Wilton—or anyone else, for that matter—hanging over her head.

She pulled a dark green windbreaker on over her shorts and T-shirt, catching her breath at the pain this movement caused her. Suddenly she was exhausted, more tired than she'd ever been in her life. She didn't want to go out into the dark night, she didn't want to be alert and wary, dealing with the guy in the leather jacket tomorrow, she didn't want to make the world's fastest getaway before Chernak heard about the deal.

She shook herself a little. *Just one more day*, she thought. *Just a few more hours, and you'll have everything you ever needed. Then you can go off and have a nice quiet nervous breakdown.*

She slipped away from the Seaside just as her neighbor broke into song: "Lonely Women Make Good Lovers."

Allegra smiled cynically and began walking. She was soaked by the time she reached the beach and paused for a moment in front of Grace's house. There were no lights on. Well, that figured. Chernak's men were professionals; they were very capable of snatching Grace without so much as disturbing a mouse. Allegra thought briefly of the other people sleeping there. None of them knew the day that lay in store for them. Would the beach house be covered with yellow "crime scene" ribbons and crawling with detectives tomorrow?

But then again, Allegra rationalized, would Chernak really kill Grace? All he'd done to Allegra was leave her with a poodle-sized bruise on her chest.

That was just a warning and you know it, a voice whispered in Allegra's mind. *Besides, Chernak knows you won't go to the police, but Grace would. She'd go in a minute. And he'll never let her do that.*

"Quiet," Allegra said out loud. The voice stopped.

Boy, she was really losing it, talking to herself and wandering around in a storm that was probably technically a hurricane or worse. She fought her way against the wind all the way to the beach stand.

She dropped to her knees and began digging. The wind whipped her long wet hair into her face, and her injured ribs protested, but she kept scraping away at the sand. She paused and pushed her hair out of her face. Her hands left long dirty streaks on her face.

Suddenly, out of nowhere, the voice in her mind came back. Only this time it was Grace's voice, gentle, lightly sarcastic, *Oh, I always want everyone to do the right thing.*

"Shut up!" Allegra whispered. She began digging again.

The voice tried to speak up again. *Oh*, it said, *I always—*

But then it stopped, because Allegra had reached the four bags of cocaine. She could hold them, feel them, dream about her future, and that silenced the voice in her head.

The membrane between Kate and the rest of the world continued to thicken. Kate could no longer hear any voices. She didn't know whether it was still storming or not. She thought of the doctor saying, *A few awaken with vague recollections of events that transpired while they were comatose. And there have been cases where comatose patients recover and claim to have seen and heard everything.* She knew she hadn't been aware of everything, but at least she hadn't felt so isolated. If only Justin would hold her hand. If only Chelsea would come back and talk to her.

No sooner had she thought of Chelsea than she saw her. Her view was that of someone hanging from the ceiling light fixture in Chelsea and Connor's bedroom. Chelsea was sitting up in bed, staring straight ahead. Connor was sleeping with his head in Chelsea's lap, his long arms circling her waist. He was snoring softly. Chelsea was stroking his carrot-colored hair and saying, "It's going to be okay, sweetheart, it's going to be okay," even though Connor was obviously in dreamland and Chelsea was speaking to herself.

Kate wanted to reach out to Chelsea. Why was she so far above her? She tried to float down from the ceiling, but suddenly she was on the beach, watching a figure in a windbreaker clutching a backpack to its middle and staggering against the wind.

My God, that's Allegra, Kate thought as

she saw the telltale auburn hair, now water-darkened to mahogany, stream out behind the figure. *What has she got in that bag? She's acting like it's the directions to the Fountain of Youth.*

Allegra looked up at where Kate hovered, but she obviously didn't see her. She was squinting in the pelting rain, looking for house numbers, obviously trying to find her way somewhere.

Lightning flashed and Kate was back indoors, in an odd, book-lined room she'd never seen before. A guy in soggy blue pajamas was curled into a ball on the bed, sobbing. He was crying so hard that his glasses were steaming up. Kate knew him from somewhere, she'd seen him once or twice, someone had talked about him, someone had said he was wonder—

And there was Grace! Kate was almost directly above her, but she could still make out the double twists of rope across Grace's thighs. And what was that she was bending over? A bottle? *No, Grace!* Kate tried to say, but as soon as she thought it, she felt herself snapping away from wherever Grace was, speeding through the darkness.

Who am I going to see next? Kate wondered. *And isn't my own life supposed to be flashing before my eyes? Not everyone else's!*

She came to a shuddering halt in the velvety blackness. *Hey*, she thought, *I'd rather be watching other people's lives than lying alone in the dark*.

"You're not alone," said a voice. A girl appeared next to her, superimposed on the darkness around her.

"Hello," Kate said. She felt only faint surprise. It was her sister, Julianna.

ELEVEN

Mr. Harriman—whose real name was Carl Carrollton—walked back into the room to find the girl passed out, slumping forward in the hardback chair. The bottle lay empty on her lap.

She had untied her legs and had apparently been working on the duct tape on her feet when she'd lost consciousness.

He closed the door behind him and knelt beside her. "Hey, beautiful," he said softly. "Looks like you had a drink after all." He patted her cheek. Her lovely dark eyes opened a slit. It took them a long time to focus.

"Hmmm?" she said sleepily.

"What have we here?" Mr. Harriman asked, holding up the ropes she had dropped to the floor. "A little escape plan?"

161

"Nooo." She could barely get the words out. Mr. Harriman leaned closer to hear. "I thought . . . we could . . . work it out. . . ."

Mr. Harriman reached in his pocket for his Swiss Army knife. He began cutting the tape that bound her feet together.

The girl leaned her head back. "Then you'll . . . let me go . . . right?" she said. "Mr. Harriman?"

"Sure thing," said Mr. Harriman, a.k.a. Carl Carrollton. He sawed away at the duct tape. He thought, *Dream on.*

Wilton's mother opened the door to his bedroom, knocking softly.

"Wilton?" she whispered. "Sweetie, you've been crying for hours."

Wilton sat up, wiping his nose on his pajama sleeve. "You could hear me?"

His mother nodded. She sat on the edge of his bed. She wore a white cotton nightgown with a little pink bow at the neckline. "What is it, darling?" she asked.

Wilton just shook his head.

"You're sure there's nothing Daddy and I can do?" his mother asked. "You can tell us anything. You know that, don't you?"

Wilton nodded, but he was thinking about how after his brother was arrested, his mother had wandered around the house, picking things up and putting them down, saying over and over to his father, "But I'm sure if they knew what a nice boy Eric is, they'd change their minds. You must call the police and tell them." Wilton had thought he would scream.

Now he looked at his mother, with her glasses and her nightgown with the pink bow, this person he loved so fiercely, and knew that he could tell her nothing.

"There's nothing you or Dad could do," he said at last.

"Well, don't you at least want to talk about it?" his mother asked. "It's breaking my heart to hear you cry."

Wilton sighed. "Mom, look—just sit here until I fall asleep, okay? Will that make you feel better?"

His mother cheered up immediately. She made him get under the covers and tucked the blankets around his chin. Then she sat next to him and held his hand.

Wilton closed his eyes, but he was miles away from sleeping. He would never sleep again. He opened one eye. His mother was looking at him, bright-eyed. "Mom," he said. "Tell me the story of how you met Dad."

"Okay," she said. She told this story about

a million times a year, requested or not, and Wilton was always soothed by her familiar rhythm and phrasing. His mother never varied.

"I had just moved into my first apartment," she said softly, stroking his hand. "I was working as a secretary and I made only seventy-five dollars a month, but believe me, I thought it was a fortune. So anyway, I had moved into my apartment and was painting the baseboards in the tiny yellow bathroom when suddenly I heard this man in the next apartment shouting, 'Help! Can anyone hear me?' "

The doorbell rang.

Wilton's mother dropped his hand.

"Ignore it," Wilton said. He felt like his heart was turning to sawdust. He knew it would be Chernak's huge henchman at the door again. What would he hand Wilton this time? A picture of Grace dead? "Keep talking, Mom."

"Wilton, we have to answer the door," his mother said. "It could only be an emergency at this hour."

"It's probably a prank," Wilton said. "I want to hear the rest of your story."

His mother hesitated. Wilton could see her wavering. He knew she resented being interrupted before she got to the part about how the man yelling for help was his father, who'd gotten his arm stuck behind the toilet when he'd reached for the toothbrush he'd dropped, and how Wilton's mother had freed him expertly by rubbing Crisco on his elbow.

The doorbell rang again.

"We have to answer it," his mother said. "Some poor soul is out in this storm—"

"Okay, let me," Wilton said quickly. He didn't want his mother offering Chernak's thug a cup of tea. He hopped out of bed and pattered down the hall. The doorbell rang again as Wilton turned the knob.

He opened the door and looked at the person standing there for a very long time. Then he said, "Do you know where to go?" in a flat voice.

Grace waited until Mr. Harriman was cutting the last shred of tape from her ankles, and then she bonked him over the head with the empty bourbon bottle.

"Huh," Mr. Harriman said thickly. His eyes rolled upward.

She hit him again.

"Hug," he said distinctly, and fell over.

In the movies, people get hit over the head once and pass out, but Grace wasn't going to trust what she'd seen in the movies. She whacked Mr. Harriman a few more times.

Actually, she should have gone by what she'd seen in the movies. Mr. Harriman would've remained unconscious for quite some time just from one slug with the bottle. As it was, her third hit with the bottle would cause him to favor his right leg for the rest of his life, and her fourth meant that he would never be able to memorize phone numbers again. She came very close to killing him, but fortunately—or unfortunately—he had a very thick skull.

Grace set the bourbon bottle on the table and pushed her bangs out of her face. She whispered an apology to the lush pathos plant that had absorbed the liquor.

She picked up Mr. Harriman's Swiss Army knife and waited, but she didn't hear footsteps or other sounds from elsewhere in the house. The storm was really whipping up now, but she didn't hesitate. She went straight to the window and tried to yank it open.

The window was painted shut and wouldn't budge. Grace went back for her old friend the bourbon bottle. Turning her face away, she raised the bottle, preparing to shatter the glass.

"I wouldn't do that if I were you," a voice said behind her.

Grace spun around. A man in an ivory suit stood in the doorway. She didn't say a word. He cocked the gun in his hand.

"Hello, Katie," Julianna said.

Kate stared at her. Julianna looked lovely, her cheeks rosy, her eyes sparkling. Thankfully, she didn't look like she had when Kate had last seen her: glassy-eyed, stiff, a thin trickle of blood at the corner of her mouth. This was the Julianna she had always known— pretty, vivacious, and oh-so-wonderfully alive.

"I'm not going to recover from this coma, am I?" Kate said. "You're here to take me somewhere, aren't you? Down a long tunnel with a light at the end?"

"You've been reading to many pop psychology books," Julianna said. She smiled her bright beautiful smile. It was their mother's smile. It was also Kate's smile, but she didn't know it.

"Well, then what are you doing here?" Kate demanded. "Why have you come if I'm not dying?"

Am I really arguing with my dead sister? Kate thought. *So many things I want to ask her, and here I am bickering with her.*

"It's okay," Julianna said. "You're just . . . in a place where I could get to you, so I came."

"Oh, I'm so glad you did," Kate said, thinking how inadequate she sounded. "I've missed you so much, I have so many things to tell you—"

"I'm afraid we don't have time," Julianna said. "You can't stay here too long."

"But I have things to tell you!"

Julianna shook her head. "No, you don't—"

"I do, I do!" Kate was frantic. "I think about you all the time! You've been gone so long, and I haven't been able to talk to you—"

"Kate, it won't do any good. What are you going to tell me—who you went to the senior prom with? Whatever you say won't be as important as you want it to be." Julianna paused. "Maybe I was wrong to bring you here. I thought it would be enough for us to see each other. But you have to go now."

"No," Kate said stubbornly.

"What?"

"No," Kate said again. "I'm not going anywhere until you tell me."

"Tell you what?"

"Why you killed yourself."

Julianna winced. "Kate, we don't have *time*. How can I make you understand that? If you don't go back now, you might not be able to go back at all."

"I'll take my chances," Kate said. "Start talking."

168

"Why don't you step away from the window?" the man in the ivory suit asked pleasantly. He waved the gun slightly. Grace moved.

"Please, do sit down," the man said. He gestured to the chair she'd been tied to.

"I'd rather stand, thank you," Grace said.

The man rolled his eyes. "Women," he said, smiling slightly. "You catch them in towels, in nightgowns, with tears drying on their faces, and still they hold on to their poise. It's amazing." He smiled again. "Very well, stand if you'd rather. You don't mind if I sit, do you?"

Grace shook her head, and the man sat in Mr. Harriman's old chair.

"I'm afraid I'll also have to ask you to put down the knife and the bottle," the man said politely. "They're not really much defense against a gun, but cornered people have been known to attempt foolish things. . . . Are you sure you won't sit down?"

Grace felt foolish standing there, so she set the knife and the bottle on the table and sat down on the edge of the hardback chair.

The man placed his gun on the table while he lit a cigarette. He saw her watching and held out the pack. She shook her head.

"So, my dear," the man began. He picked

the gun up again. "What have you done to poor Carl here?" He leaned down and felt Mr. Harriman's thick neck for a pulse without much interest. "Well, you haven't killed him, at any rate." He glanced at her with real interest. "Well?" he prompted.

"Well, what?"

"What did you do to Carl?"

"Oh . . . I, uh, hit him with the bourbon bottle."

"Mmm." The man took a drag off his cigarette. "Well, I'll be discreet and not inquire what crazy high jinks you and Carl were up to that involved bourbon."

"Thank you," Grace said sarcastically.

"My dear," the man began. "I'm sorry, what is your name?"

"You kidnapped me and you don't know my name?" Grace asked.

The man shrugged. "Your kidnapping was nothing personal, I assure you. You just happened to be boyfriend-girlfriend with the wrong young man."

Grace almost smiled. She couldn't believe he'd said *boyfriend-girlfriend*.

"So," the man continued. "Your name, please, unless you'd rather not. . . . Is it a secret? Do I have a Rockefeller here? Should I demand a higher ransom?"

Grace kept watching the gun. "My name is Grace," she said at last.

"Grace . . ." the man tried it out. "Pretty name."

She shrugged. "What's your name?" she asked.

His eyes sparkled. "You got kidnapped by me and you don't even know my name?"

Grace looked at him stonily, but he only laughed. "My name is Trevor Chernak," he said, watching her carefully. Her eyes widened. "I can see my name means something to you."

"You're the one . . . Kate and Justin . . . and Allegra!" Grace couldn't think coherently. "Why, I gave Allegra money."

"Did you?" Chernak shrugged. "Well, nothing to be ashamed of. She can be very persuasive." He exhaled smoke, his eyes cold and remote. "In fact, she and I have some unfinished business to settle on that score."

"So . . ." Grace hesitated.

Chernak smiled again. "Why don't you call me Mr. Chernak, Grace? Respect for your elders and all that. And do relax and let your shoulders touch the back of that chair. It makes me nervous just to look at you."

"Mr. Chernak," Grace said. "What is it? What do you want from me?"

"Oh, it's a long story," Chernak said, stubbing out his cigarette. "Wilton has something that belongs to me. I thought he might return it in exchange for you, but it appears I was wrong." He looked at his watch. "Though I've sent someone round to check on him, so there's still hope for an eleventh-hour reprieve."

Grace crossed her arms. "There's not going to be an eleventh-hour reprieve for me, whether Wilton coughs up what you want or not," she said.

Chernak raised his eyebrows. "You must watch a lot of television," he said. "Or read a lot of detective stories."

"Some of both," Grace said, disconcerted.

He smiled. "Marvelous what you can learn from books, isn't it?" he asked. "Well, you're quite right, I'm afraid. I can't just let you go." He looked at his watch again. "But no need to make your demise even more untimely, is there? And certainly no need to leave you in suspense. Let's wait and see if good ol' Wilton pulls through for you."

"Yes, let's," Grace said. A vein was beginning to pulse in her forehead, and a blood vessel had swollen in her right eye. She began to believe that she would die here.

TWELVE

Chelsea, who'd slept for a grand total of maybe ten seconds, woke with a start. She punched Connor in the arm.

"Kate's in danger," she said. "We have to go to the hospital."

"I'm driving," Connor said instantly.

"No, I am," Chelsea said. She jumped out of bed and pulled on a pale blue sundress.

Connor dragged on a pair of jeans and, bare-chested, raced to the living room for the car keys. Behind him, Chelsea held up her hand, car keys dangling from a finger. How did she move so fast? She turned and began walking for the door.

"Sweetheart," Connor said, pulling on a T-shirt as he followed her. "Our car insurance is going to go up if you drive as fast as you walk. Holy mother of God!" he said when she opened the door and he glimpsed the storm outside.

Chelsea ran down the stairs. Connor followed, barefoot. He caught her arm. "We have to go back for jackets or umbrellas or something!" he shouted over the wind.

She shook her head. "No time," she said. "Kate's in danger."

Connor shook her shoulders. "Chelsea, she's in the hospital. What's going to happen to her there?"

She looked at him, her huge brown eyes filling with tears. "I can't explain it. We have to *go*."

"Okay, sweetheart, okay," Connor said.

Together they sprinted across the parking lot, both drenched before they reached the car. Chelsea slid behind the wheel and shoved the key into the ignition. Connor wrenched open the passenger door.

"Chels—"

"We have to *go*."

"Yes, darling, but I have this desire to get there alive." He took a look at the determined frown on her face and buckled his seat belt. "Gentlemen, start your engines," he said.

They were across the parking lot and

down the street before the words were out of his mouth.

• • •

Bert, the man Chernak had sent round to check on Wilton, was having his hair toweled dry by Wilton's mother.

"There," she said, standing behind him, patting at his ears with a fluffy pink towel. Bert was sitting at the kitchen table. "Now maybe you won't get pneumonia. Are you sure I can't put your clothes in the dryer?"

"I'm sure," Bert said. "Where did you say Wilton is?"

"I didn't say where he is, because I don't *know* where he is," Wilton's mother said. "The doorbell rings and away he goes, off like a shot, without a word to me." She studied Bert. "You say you're a friend of his?"

"Yes, we lived in the same dorm," said Bert, who was thirty-eight years old. He didn't think that Wilton's mother was tracking this conversation very closely.

"Really? I wouldn't have figured you for a college man, if you don't mind my saying so," Wilton's mother said. "In fact, at first I thought you were a friend of my *other* son. He—mixed with a different crowd than Wilton."

They looked at each other across the table. Wilton's mother smiled. "How about a cup of cocoa?" she asked.

Bert paused. "That would be lovely," he said.

• • •

Julianna looked exasperated. "Kate, you have to go. Now."

"Tell me," Kate said.

Julianna spoke rapidly. "Can't you feel something pulling at you? That means you should go. You can't stay here with me."

"So then tell me!"

Julianna bit her lip. "It wasn't like there was a reason, Kate." Her voice was hurried. "I wasn't happy, I was never—at peace."

"But if you'd told us—"

"Told you I wasn't happy? Were you going to *make* me happy?" Julianna raised an eyebrow. "I thought you knew better than that."

"But—but—"

"I thought I could make myself happy, and get away from the pain," Julianna said. "And I got away from the pain, but . . ." Suddenly she smiled, wryly, ironically. "You can be happy like I never could. So now, go! Go, you idiot, before we run out of time."

"But maybe I should stay. You could be happy if I—" Kate began.

"I am happy, Kate!" Julianna protested.

"You can be happy with Justin—why can't you see that?"

"Wait, I have to kiss you good-bye—"

"We can't touch because we're not really here," Julianna said. "Try it."

Kate leaned forward to embrace her sister and found herself spiraling through the darkness again. *No!* she screamed. *No! I don't want to leave!*

Chernak and Grace were sharing the last cigarette in the pack.

"If I were truly a gentleman, I would give it to you," he said with a shrug. "But, well, we both know that I'm not a gentleman."

Grace said nothing. She took a long drag off the cigarette. She didn't usually smoke, but she figured she was probably going to be dead in a few hours, so why not? It was a mistake, though. It only made her think of long nights in smoky bars, and that made her want a drink.

Chernak checked his watch. "Where is Bert?" he asked irritably. (Bert was, at that moment, hearing the story of how Wilton's parents met.)

Grace shrugged. "Maybe Wilton killed him," she said sarcastically, her voice throaty from the cigarette.

Chernak laughed, his black eyes dancing. "Oh, I don't think he's nearly as resourceful as you. Speaking of which, when do you think our large friend here will be reviving?" He touched Mr. Harriman's inert body with the toe of his wingtip.

Grace shrugged. "I don't care," she said.

Chernak watched her, his eyes bright. "Doesn't it bother you that your boyfriend hasn't agreed to pay the ransom?"

"I'm sure he has his reasons."

Chernak continued to study her. "Well, you're very forgiving," he said.

"It's not a matter of forgiveness," Grace said. "You've already said you can't let me go, and I'm sure if Wilton handed over whatever it is, you'd just kill us both."

"True enough," Chernak said. "Still, I must say that if you were my girlfriend, I would be a little more attentive."

Grace said nothing. *Ah, the obligatory pass*, she thought. *I wondered when that was coming.*

"You are extraordinarily lovely," Chernak said. "But I suppose you know that. Well, perhaps I should tell you anyway. It will pass the time, and women like compliments. . . . You have very pretty hair, and a lovely mouth—when you're not frowning at me, that is—and of course, your figure in that gown is exceptional. But your eyes, my dear, are certainly your fortune. They have so much fire and spirit. It makes me wonder exactly what you would do if I were to take you in my arms." He smiled gently.

Grace looked at him. She leaned forward and spoke softly. "If you were to take me in your arms, I would hurt you worse than I hurt Mr. Harriman," she said, and she meant it.

Kate realized she was back in her hospital bed. Outside it was still storming.

She turned her face to the side. *Julianna*, she thought. *Oh, Julianna . . .*

Very quietly she began to cry. A tear slid out of the corner of her eye and down her cheek, wetting the pillow. Kate froze.

She was crying. She could feel herself crying. She was awake, back in the real world. She tried to laugh through her tears.

She twisted her head the other way and saw—Justin. Oh, so there he was, asleep in a chair next to her, looking like he'd been run over by a tractor. She'd been having all those weird dreams about him dying and wondering where he was, and he'd been right next to her all the time.

She tried to say his name, but her throat

was too dry. It took her several tries, and then she finally whispered, "Justin?"

His eyes snapped open—his poor, bloodshot, wild eyes—and rested on hers. "Oh, my God," he said.

He was out of the chair in a second, sitting on the edge of her bed. "Kate, you're back, oh, Kate, you came back." He was babbling, but she didn't care.

Kate tried to lift her hand off the bed. Justin saw the movement. "What?" he asked. "What do you want? Water?"

From the moment Justin said the word *water*, Kate's throat felt like it was on fire. She nodded. He ran to the bathroom and came back with a glass of water.

"Careful, just a little," he said, holding the glass to her lips.

Kate swallowed, and was lost for a moment in the cool, mossy joy of it. Her throat had never been this dry in her life. She looked at Justin gratefully. He gave her another sip. Kate closed her eyes. Oh, the wet green taste of it. Wonderful. She would drink ten gallons of water a day for the rest of life. She took another sip and opened her eyes.

"Thanks," she whispered.

"You're welcome." Justin smoothed her

hair off her forehead.

"But that's not actually what I wanted," Kate said softly.

"No?" Justin smiled. "You seemed to be pretty thirsty."

She smiled weakly. "I actually wanted to touch you," she said.

"Oh," Justin said. "Well, that can be arranged."

He pulled her close to him very gently and buried his face in her neck. Kate curled an arm around his neck, still faintly surprised that she could move.

"Oh, Justin," she said. Her voice was getting stronger, too. "I was so afraid you were dying."

"You were afraid *I* was dying?' Justin said. "How do you think I felt?"

Kate pulled away slightly and looked at him. "You don't understand,"; she said, a tiny frown between her eyes. "I kept having these dreams that you were in danger, and I was so scared that I would never get the chance to tell you how much I loved you."

"You're a nut," Justin said kindly. "You're in a coma, worrying about me. That's crazy."

"I suppose. . . ." Kate was still frowning, preoccupied.

"Hey," Justin said softly. "Hey, Katie, think

what it was like for me. You *were* in danger, and I hadn't told you how I felt. I hadn't *begun* to tell you how I felt."

Kate looked at him and smiled gently. *He's going to tell me he loves me*, she thought.

"Marry me," Justin said.

Behind him the door sprang open, and Chelsea catapulted through like a small fury.

The doorbell rang.

"At last," Chernak said. "Bert must be back." He stood up and gestured at her with the gun. "Come with me."

Chernak and Grace walked through the beach house, Chernak keeping an iron grip on her arm. The doorbell rang again.

Chernak held a finger to his lips and peered through the peephole. He grinned at Grace. "Your knight in shining armor," he said. He threw open the door.

Wilton stood on the porch, four bags of white powder in his hands. He was wearing pajamas, soaked to the skin, looking even skinnier and paler than usual. There were large dark smudges under his eyes. Grace's heart sang at the sight of him, even though she knew it meant that Chernak would kill them both.

"Wilton," Chernak said. "How nice of you

to show up at long last. Poor Grace has been biting her fingernails. Won't you come in?"

Suddenly the yard outside flooded with spotlights. Two state troopers stepped out from either side of Wilton, their guns drawn. Grace thought she glimpsed Allegra standing near a police car.

"Why, thank you, Mr. Chernak," one of the troopers said, matching Chernak's mocking tone. "Don't mind if we do."

"So then," Wilton's mother was saying, "he asked me to go bowling, and I thought it was a date and got very excited. I spent all afternoon taking a bubble bath and painting my toenails and everything. But it turned out that he'd only wanted me to join his bowling team, and when I went out to get in the car, it was filled with people."

"So what happened?" Bert asked.

"Oh, well, eventually we went on a real date and got married and had Wilton and Eric."

"No, I mean, what happened when you saw the car filled with people?" Bert said. "Did you start crying and run into the bathroom?"

"No, though I certainly felt like it. I'm sure my face just fell," Wilton's mother said musingly. "Would you like some more marshmallows?"

"No, thank you," Bert said. He stood up heavily. "I think I should be going."

"But you haven't even seen Wilton yet," Wilton's mother protested.

"I think maybe it's best for Wilton if I don't see him," Bert said quietly.

"Oh," Wilton's mother said softly. "I was hoping that I was—that you really were a friend of his from college."

Bert shook his head.

Wilton's mother smiled. "Wait just a minute," she said. She slipped into the kitchen and came back with a brown paper bag. It was the lunch she had made for Wilton to take with him to work the next day.

Bert ate the turkey sandwich as he sped south in his car. In the bottom of the lunch bag was a Hershey kiss with a note folded around it. *Darling,* the note read, *Things will look up.* The note had been written for Wilton, of course, but it worked just fine on Bert. He ate the chocolate kiss and put the note in his pocket, whistling as he drove across the state line.

THIRTEEN

Chelsea bustled over to the bed. "Well, her eyes are open," she said clinically. "That's a good sign, at least."

"I'm awake," Kate said.

Chelsea screamed. Everyone jumped.

"Oh, my God," Chelsea whispered, her hand over her mouth. "You scared me."

Kate smiled faintly. "Sorry."

With a small sob, Chelsea hurled herself into Kate's arms, neatly dislodging Justin. "I was so *worried*," she wailed. "I was so *scared*."

"Shhh," Kate said softly. She smiled at Connor and Justin over Chelsea's head. "It's okay now, Chels, it's okay."

Chelsea snuffled against Kate's neck.

A doctor rushed into the room. "Good God,

what happened?" he asked. "I heard someone screaming from halfway down the hall."

Chelsea disentangled herself from Kate and stood up. "That was me," she said. "I'm sorry." She took a Kleenex from the box by the bed and blew her nose.

"Well, try to control yourself, young lady," the doctor said. "This is a hospital. Now, if you folks will excuse us, I'd like to examine Kate, and then she'll need to sleep."

"I don't want to sleep," Kate protested. "I've been sleeping for hours."

"Not sleeping—comatose," the doctor corrected. "Don't worry, you won't slip back into a coma, I promise."

"Are my parents here?" Kate asked.

"I convinced them to go to a hotel," the doctor said. "Shall I call them, or would you like to do that yourself?"

"Oh, I want to call," Kate said.

"Okay, I'll have a nurse bring the number, but don't have them rush over here in this storm," the doctor said. "You're going to be around for a long time, I suspect, and we don't need a car crash in this storm."

"Amen," Connor murmured under his breath.

Chelsea lingered, holding Kate's hand.

"Come on, Chelsea," Connor said. "You

only have nine months of training time before the Indy 500."

Reluctantly, Chelsea let go of Kate's hand. She leaned forward and whispered, "I love you," in Kate's ear.

"Me, too," Kate whispered, and then the doctor shepherded Chelsea, Connor, and Justin from the room. Kate's eyes met Justin's as he left. When would they be alone?

It took forever for the cops to question everyone. They swarmed over the house, making pot after pot of coffee, deposing people at the kitchen table. They called an ambulance for Mr. Harriman, who still hadn't stirred.

One of the paramedics whistled. He was the same beefy guy who'd attended to Kate. "What happened to this guy?"

"Fight with a bourbon bottle," one of the cops told him.

The beefy paramedic shook his head. "Jeez, what does the other guy look like?" It took both paramedics and two cops to haul Mr. Harriman's bulk out to the ambulance.

They took Chernak away in handcuffs. He asked Grace if she would visit him in prison. She said sarcastically that she would think about it.

Allegra sat next to Grace on the sofa while

the police took Wilton's statement. Allegra's face was streaked with dirt, and her long auburn hair hung in hopeless tangles. Yet she was beautiful.

"So," Allegra said. "I did the right thing after all."

"I see," Grace said. "Do you—Are you going to be arrested?"

Allegra shook her head. "No. I'm helping them set up a sting operation on the beach tomorrow. I guess if I pull that off and nobody tracks me down and kills me, I'll be a free agent."

"Oh," Grace said.

"Are you—okay?" Allegra asked.

Grace ran a hand through her hair. "I've been better."

"You have a red spot in one of your eyes," Allegra said tactlessly.

Grace began laughing.

"What?" Allegra said.

"Do me a favor," Grace said.

"Sure."

"Can you really make yourself cry on command?"

Allegra blinked. Her green eyes filled with tears. She blinked again. They were gone.

Grace laughed harder. "Do it again. Oh, please, do it again."

"Watch, I can make my chin tremble, too," Allegra said.

"Okay, cry," Grace said.

Tears gathered on Allegra's lashes.

"Now stop."

No tears fell. "And the best part is that my nose never runs," Allegra said, smiling.

"Water, please," Grace said. Obediently, Allegra began to cry. Grace felt as though she would never get tired of this game.

Five minutes later, when the cops wanted to take Grace's statement, she and Allegra were laughing so hard they couldn't speak.

"Water," Grace gasped as one of the detectives grasped her arm. "Water."

"What?" he said. "You want a drink?"

The doctor examined Kate, shining a light in her eyes, taking her blood pressure, listening to her lungs.

Then he sat in the chair beside her bed and clasped his hands behind his head. "I have some questions for you," he said. "What's your name?"

"Kate Quinn."

"What day is today?"

"I don't know. . . ."

"That's okay, that's normal. What's your mother's maiden name?"

189

"Etheridge."

"How many pennies in a dollar?"

"A hundred?"

"Good. How many quarters?"

"Four."

"Who's your best friend?"

"Chelsea Len—Riordan."

"How many brothers and sisters do you have?"

Kate frowned.

"Kate?" the doctor said.

You can be happy with Justin—why can't you see that?

"Kate?"

"One—one," she stammered. "Julianna."

"Good girl. What's the square root of nine?"

"Umm . . . I can't remember."

"Where are you?

"The hospital."

"But which city?"

"Ocean City."

"What's the richest city in the world?"

"What?"

"Generosity," the doctor smiled. "That's a joke."

"Oh," Kate said. She smiled.

"You're in very good shape for having sustained such a serious head injury," the doctor said. "You have almost no memory loss. A little shaky on numbers, but that'll come back." He stood up. "I'm going to send a nurse in with a sedative. I want you to take it as soon as you've spoken to your parents. I'll see you on rounds tomorrow."

"Okay," Kate said. "Doctor?"

He turned.

"I want to tell you—" Kate paused. "I could hear things while I was comatose."

"Really?"

"Yes. . . . I heard you and Chelsea talking about what I could or couldn't hear," Kate said. She cleared her throat. "Anyway, I wanted you to know that you're right to encourage people to talk to comatose patients."

He looked a little surprised, then thoughtful. "Thank you for telling me that, Kate," he said.

"You're welcome," she said. "Will you let my boyfriend come in to say good night?"

"Sure," he said. "Just for a minute, though."

Justin came through the door slowly. He was stupid with sleep. He came over and lay down on the bed with her. She put her arms around him.

"Yes," she whispered.

Justin pulled away and looked at her.

"Yes," she said again. "Yes, yes, yes."

Justin smiled, and it was a beautiful smile despite the bloodshot eyes, the stubbly beard, the wild-man-of-Borneo hair.

He dropped his head onto her chest and said something. It could have been "Great" or it could have been "Good night." Kate never found out, not that she cared.

After the detectives had questioned her and given her a glass of water that she didn't really want, Grace found herself talking to Wilton on the deck of Chernak's beach house. The storm had finally blown over, and dawn was beginning to break through.

"Now you know why I was so preoccupied," Wilton said.

Grace nodded. "I wish you'd told me."

"Well, I didn't want to drag you into this mess," Wilton said. "And that's exactly what happened."

"Wilton, this isn't your fault," Grace said. "I wish you'd trusted me enough to tell me, is all."

Wilton looked surprised. "Of course I trust you."

She shook her head. "But you didn't tell me anything important," she said.

Wilton lowered his head and looked her in

the eye. "I told you I loved you," he said. "Doesn't that count?"

Grace bit her lip. She smiled half a smile.

Wilton put his hand on her shoulder. "I called Bo and Roan to tell them that you were okay and they told me that Kate's come out of her coma. She's going to be fine."

"Oh," Grace breathed. "Oh, that's wonderful."

"I called my parents, too—oh, yikes," he said suddenly.

"What?"

"I should warn you, you're going to get this letter from my mother, inviting you to Sunday dinner," Wilton said, mortified. "You don't have to come if you don't want to—"

"Oh, I wouldn't miss it for the world," Grace said. She put her arms around him. She rested her nose against his chest, and suddenly she began laughing.

"What is it?" Wilton said.

"I was about to tell you that I loved you when I realized you were wearing jammies with horses embroidered on them," Grace said. She started to laugh, and then cry, and then laugh again. She wondered if her emotions would ever straighten out.

Wilton didn't say anything. He just held her and beamed.

• • •

Chelsea and Connor walked into their apartment, shed their clothes, and fell into bed.

"Wow," Chelsea said. "What a day. Are you going to put this into your novel?"

"I don't know yet," Connor said, pulling her close to him. "So where were we about twenty hours ago? Weren't you mad at me?"

"Oh, probably," Chelsea said, smiling.

"Don't be mad," Connor said softly, already slipping into sleep.

"Don't worry," Chelsea said, smoothing Connor's hair away from his face. And watching him sleep, she handed him her heart all over again, just like that.